The Captain and Mrs. Vye

BOOK 1 IN THE WIVES OF OLD CAPE MAY SERIES OF WOMEN'S FICTION

MARYANN DIORIO

The Captain and Mrs. Vye

by MaryAnn Diorio

The maid's face broke into a broad grin. "Oh, Mrs. Vye! There is no finer mistress than yourself. I'm much obliged to you."

Loretta placed her index finger on her chin. "I have an even better idea. Why don't you leave now? I'll take care of everything. It's been a long time since I've had the pleasure of serving dinner to my husband. Besides, he will be leaving tomorrow for Liverpool. I think it would be rather enjoyable to wait on him this evening."

A shadow passed over Molly's face. "The master will be leavin' tomorrow?"

Loretta's heart grew heavy. "Yes, I'm afraid so. And I don't know how long he will be gone."

"I'm sorry, ma'am." Molly frowned.

"I am, too. So very sorry. I fear I am quite incapable of managing without him. Mr. Vye is the decision-maker in our marriage. I simply follow his lead."

Molly furrowed her brow. "But, ma'am, may I be so bold as to venture an opinion?"

"Of course, my dear."

Molly squared her jaw. "Women can be quite as competent as men. And, if I daresay, perhaps even more so."

Loretta raised an eyebrow. "Ah, my dear Molly, you've been listening to those shouting women with their new-fangled ideas about our fair gender. What do they call themselves? Suffragists? Or something of the sort? Whatever their name, they are not only affirming their equality with men–they are trying to usurp their position." Loretta sighed. "Besides, the Good Book says that women must be submissive."

Molly's face flushed. "Not meanin' any disrespect, ma'am, but women are, indeed, equal to men, in value if not in function. And, as for submission, there's a difference between submittin' and submergin' oneself to the point of denying who one is."

Loretta sighed. "Well, I suppose so. But as far as competence in making major decisions, I would say that men are much the wiser."

Molly's face twitched before she straightened out her expression. "Beggin' your pardon, Mrs. Vye, but I think it's the other way around. Seems as though me dad relies on me mum pretty much for everything. Why, he can't even find his socks unless she comes to his rescue." Molly giggled. "Anyway, we can agree to disagree agreeably."

Loretta laughed. "That we can, dear Molly. That we can."

Molly changed the subject. "What about Mr. Vye's birthday party, ma'am? Not meanin' any disrespect, but should he not be present at his own party?"

"Indeed, he should." A hint of bitterness rode on the back of Loretta's words. "But certain things in life cannot be controlled. They must simply be accepted."

Molly tilted her head. "That may be so, ma'am. But a lass is not compelled to accept everything that crosses her path. She has the ability to change some things."

Loretta looked away. At one time, she herself had been as feisty and free as Molly. Once she, too, had considered herself capable and competent. But that was before her parents died. Mama had always told her she could do anything she put her mind to. Papa had encouraged her to pursue her dreams. What had changed? Had her parents' tragic death in a carriage accident and her subsequent move to live with Aunt Martha and Uncle Malcolm at the tender age of eight so crushed Loretta's spirit that she had lost her will to fight?

She gave Molly a motherly smile. "One day you'll understand. But for now, run along. And make sure you bring that beau of yours to meet me. He requires my approval, you know."

Molly laughed. "Yes, Mrs. Vye. I will bring Sean by on the morrow, if you'd like."

"Yes, that would be perfect. After Mr. Vye has left, I will need some distraction to ease my sorrow."

And after that?

Loretta put her hand to her chest in a vain attempt to quell the gnawing ache.

* * *

Tuesday morning, February 18, 1873

Jeremiah Collins unlocked the door between his living quarters and the front part of his fishing supply store. Today was the third anniversary of its opening, and he'd planned a celebration to thank his faithful customers for their support and to attract new customers.

Running a store was quite different from plying the high seas seeking his fortune in scaly silver, as he'd done for twenty-five years. After he'd married his beloved Anna Mae, he'd had to leave her behind for days, even weeks at a time.

A lump formed in his throat at the memory of her.

The injury he'd sustained when an anchor had fallen on his foot had forced him to leave behind his profession as a North Atlantic trawler captain to seek an easier trade. A constant limp attested to the brutal, if necessary, exchange.

He'd grown accustomed to the slower-paced life, yet, truth be told, he missed the adventure and excitement—and maybe even the danger—of the hunt.

He entered the front of the store, gently closing the door behind him. The musty smell of closed quarters struck his nostrils, eliciting a cough. He pulled up the shade and turned the sign in the window to indicate the store was open for business.

Burrows, his calico cat, greeted him with a loud purr and a rub against the shin.

Jeremiah reached down to scratch her neck. "Good morning, Burrows. I see you're up bright and early."

The cat looked up with questioning eyes.

"I know. I know. You're wanting your breakfast. Give a man a minute to settle in, will you?' He sighed. "You're like every other woman I know. Demanding and manipulative. Except for Anna Mae. I'm glad you're only a cat." Jeremiah chuckled.

Burrows hunched her back and hissed.

"See? Just as I said. Demanding and manipulative."

With a huff, Jeremiah made his way to the tiny kitchen at the back of the store. He reached into a cupboard, withdrew a small handful of scraps, and placed them in Burrows's bowl. "Here you go. Now, that should hold you over for a good while—at least, until I get myself settled."

Jeremiah put on a pot of coffee and then went to the front of the store. Despite the cold temperatures, the day was brisk and clear. That meant people would be encouraged to come out and celebrate. He'd planned a few games for the children and a few prizes for the adults. He'd also put several items on sale.

As he placed the discounted items on the counter, the bell over the front door sounded.

"Mornin', Jeremiah." Tom Brogan entered with a smile.

"Well, if it isn't my favorite customer." Jeremiah grinned.

"Aw, you say that to every customer."

Jeremiah feigned insult. "I do not."

"It don't matter, my friend. I know I'm your favorite."

"Well, I must be doing something right for you to feel that way."

Tom gave Jeremiah a pat on the back. "You and I have been friends for comin' up on three years now, Jeremiah. You know I love joshin' you."

Jeremiah chuckled. "Yes, I know." He put his hands on his hips. "How about a cup of coffee? I just brewed it."

"I smelled the aroma as soon as I walked in. A cup would suit me just fine."

Jeremiah motioned to Tom to follow him to the back of the store. After preparing two cups of coffee, Jeremiah invited Tom to sit at the small kitchen table.

Jeremiah stretched his long legs in front of him, being careful to position his limp leg underneath his good one.

Tom took a sip of his coffee. "I got somethin' to show you." He withdrew a small knife from the back pocket of his trousers. "Got meself this here knife for scalin' fish. Even had my initials engraved on it." He handed the knife to Jeremiah.

Jeremiah turned it over in his hand a few times, examining its intricacies. "Nice-lookin' knife. Have you tried it out yet?" He handed the knife back to Tom.

"Yeah. Caught some flounder yesterday and skinned it with this knife. Did a pretty good job."

"A pocket knife is a handy tool to carry."

Tom replaced the knife in his back pocket. "So are you ready for the celebration?"

"I think so. The event will start at ten o'clock this morning and run until four o'clock this afternoon. I hope you can stick around for part of the time, at least."

"I plan to. If you need any help settin' up or with the customers, I'm available until noon."

"Well, that's mighty generous of you, Tom."

Tom looked around the store. “Seems to me you could be usin' a woman's touch in here.”

Jeremiah furrowed his brows. “What do you mean?”

“Well, I don't see any flowers anywhere.”

Jeremiah smirked. “Tom, this is a fishing supply store, not a flower shop.”

“I know. But ain't the men bringin' their families today?”

“Yes.”

“Well, I don't know of a woman alive who prefers the smell of fish to the smell of flowers.”

“But the women don't shop here. Their men do.”

“But the women influence their men. And you can be sure that if a woman likes your store, she'll be tellin' her lady friends who'll be tellin' their husbands.”

Jeremiah scratched his head. “I should put you in charge of advertising.”

Tom laughed. “If I ever need a job, I'll be sure to come to you.”

Jeremiah gulped the last swallow of his coffee and rose. “Well, I'd better get to work. Ten o'clock will be here soon enough. How about giving me a hand moving the table out front to the center of the room? I have some free information for people to take as they come in.”

Was Tom right about a woman's touch? He hadn't known a woman's touch since his beloved Anna Mae had passed away during childbirth, their only child dying with her. His heart twisted at the agonizing memory.

The worst of it was that he'd been at sea and had not even been able to say goodbye. He'd never risk that sort of pain again.

Tuesday morning, February 18, 1873

Loretta squeezed the tear-soaked handkerchief in her right hand. The first light of dawn filtered through her bedroom window. She stood at the foot of the four-poster bed in their bedroom as Edward secured his luggage.

"Oh, Edward! I wish you didn't have to go."

He straightened and took her gently by the shoulders. "But I must, darling. It is a matter of the utmost importance."

She rubbed her nostrils with her handkerchief. "When will you return?"

"If all goes well, I shan't be more than a fortnight

in England, my dear. Including my time at sea, I shouldn't be away more than a month."

"A month! Oh, Edward, a month seems like an eternity."

He wiped a tear from her eye with his thumb. "But it isn't, darling. When I return, I shall take you for a carriage ride along the beach followed by dinner at Congress Hall. How does that sound?"

She angled away from him and crossed her arms. "It sounds totally uninteresting."

He turned her toward himself. "Then I shall think of something more interesting while I am gone." He gave her a peck on the cheek and grew serious. "Loretta, if I do not attend to the situation in Liverpool, we could fall into bankruptcy."

Loretta's muscles froze. "What are you saying?"

"I'm saying that our entire fortune rests on the success of this trip."

Her insides tightened. "Our entire fortune?"

He released her and looked her in the eye. "Yes, our entire fortune."

"But, Edward, how did it come to this?"

He cupped her face in his hands. "Loretta darling, I don't have time at the moment to explain all the details. But I shall upon my return. My carriage will arrive momentarily. I need to carry my luggage to the front door."

Loretta's heart plummeted to her feet. "I shall see you off, then. Please do write while you're gone."

"Most certainly, darling, I shall write. But my letters may reach you after I return." He caressed her cheek. "Now, let me give you a proper farewell kiss and then I must be gone." Edward kissed her soundly.

The touch of his lips upon hers warmed her blood. Oh, how she would miss him!

"Enjoy my birthday party." He chuckled.

"I will be a good hostess, but I cannot promise you that I will enjoy your birthday party without you." How he could think otherwise lay beyond her comprehension.

"And don't fret while I'm gone, do you hear?"

"That will be easier said than done, Edward. You know me. I depend too much on you."

"That you do, my dear. That you do." He laughed. "But I must confess that I rather enjoy your need of me."

Her body stiffened. Edward might enjoy it, but she certainly didn't. Ever since her parents died, depending on others had been the story of her life. She hated that it was so. Even while living with cruel Aunt Martha and

Uncle Malcolm, she'd despised the thought of having to depend on them for her sustenance. She'd vowed that when she grew up, she'd depend on no one but herself. She would call the plays for her own life, her own way.

Yet her vow had fallen by the wayside, for here she was, depending on Edward. Despite his kindness and generosity, being beholden to him for her every need was somehow beneath her dignity. Not that he treated her disrespectfully, but he was fully aware of his financial power over her.

And so was she.

For once, she wanted to be free. Self-sufficient. In need of nothing and no one. Why should a woman have to depend on a man for her every need? Indeed, the Proverbs 31 woman owned her own business. Perhaps one day she would too.

Loretta sighed. A caged bird needed to fly.

She stifled the annoyance. "Please take care of yourself while you're gone, Edward."

"By all means. There's nothing like British tea and crumpets to strengthen one's body and soul." Edward liked to tease her during difficult moments. It was his way of relieving the tension.

She placed a hand on his chest. "Be sure to include some brisket and roasted potatoes as well." Her attempt at humor paled against his. Humor for a breaking heart was like putting salt on a wound. Choking back tears, Loretta buried her head in Edward's chest. “I'll be eagerly awaiting your return.”

He stroked her hair. “I will as well, my dear, though I’m relieved that Molly will be staying with you until I return.”

Loretta nodded. Having a companion would ease her loneliness, not to mention quell her fear. Ever since her parents’ death, she found herself in dread of the worst that could happen.

At the sound of the oncoming carriage outside, Edward took a step backward. “The carriage has arrived. I really must be going.” He picked up his luggage.

Her heart overflowing with misgivings, Loretta accompanied him down the staircase to the front door.

He gave her one last perfunctory kiss and was out the door.

From the front porch, Loretta's gaze followed the carriage to the end of the driveway until it disappeared completely.

She turned back toward the front door, a cold sensation settling in the pit of her stomach.

Chapter Two

Thursday, February 20, 1873

The day after Edward's departure from New York—Loretta wended her way through tree-lined streets toward the church where her knitting circle met every Thursday morning. She approached the little church with anticipation, the church that she and Edward had attended since their wedding nineteen years earlier. The women in her knitting circle were her closest friends. Women who'd been through a lot in life. Women she could count on to give her good advice. She always looked forward to being with them.

She hastened up the short walkway to the front door. At this time of year, the trees were bare, but in a few short weeks, their branches would blossom with the loveliest of maple leaves. She smiled at the thought. Spring always gave her new life. New hope.

But would it be different this spring after Edward's trip? He'd been gone only two days, yet it seemed like forever. By now, he was on the high seas, on his way to Liverpool. He'd promised to telegraph her upon his arrival, which would not be for another week at least, depending on the tailwinds.

Her knitting bag hanging from her arm, she entered the vestibule. The wooden structure was one of the first churches built in Cape May. Its stained-glass windows had been brought to America by early settlers from Scotland. Loretta loved the way the sunshine streamed through the panes, creating a prism of vibrant color that shimmered across the pews.

She headed for the rear of the building to the Sunday school room. A scraping of wooden chairs as she approached told her someone had already arrived.

"Good morning, Loretta." Clarissa Steubens looked up from arranging the chairs around the table and broke into a smile. In her early sixties, Clarissa was like a mother to Loretta. "It's good to see you, my dear."

"Good morning, Clarissa. It's good to see you, too." Loretta chose her usual seat in front of the window and placed her items on it. So far, only she and Clarissa had arrived. “How are you this week?”

“I can't complain. I planted some seedlings indoors yesterday to prepare for replanting outdoors in the spring. Here's hoping they will sprout.”

Loretta smiled. “You're the consummate gardener. I've always admired that about you.”

“Why, thank you. And what about you? How was your week? And how are plans coming along for Edward's birthday party?”

Loretta settled into her chair and sighed. “Well, Edward left for England this week on business, so he won't be attending his birthday party.”

“Oh?” Clarissa took the chair beside her.

“Yes. He said it was urgent.” Loretta choked back tears. “He said there'd been a sudden negative turn of events in our finances, and he had to make the trip.”

“I'm so sorry.” Clarissa placed a hand on Loretta's arm. “You seem upset.”

“Truth be told, I am. Quite upset.”

“Well, I hope that being with us today will encourage you.”

“You ladies are about the only thing at the moment that can encourage me.”

Clarissa smiled. “Don't forget Jesus. He's always with you. Encourage yourself in Him.” Clarissa had a special way of always pointing people to Jesus. At times, Loretta found it annoying, as it seemed to minimize a person's feelings. But today she found it strangely comforting.

Miriam Goldstein was next to arrive, followed by Ebony Philips.

"Shalom, everyone!" Miriam greeted her friends as she located her chair.

Loretta had marveled at Miriam's conversion to Christianity only a year before. The dear Jewish woman had suffered much at the hands of her family and fellow Jews as a result. Yet she'd remained strong in her commitment to her Messiah.

Ebony smiled, displaying perfectly straight white teeth, sparkling against her creamy chocolate skin. Ebony could make the darkest place shine bright with the love of Christ. "Praise the Lord and glory to God. We made it through another week."

Loretta looked up. "Well, barely."

Ebony took the chair to Loretta's left and scrunched her brows. "What do you mean 'barely'?"

Loretta filled her in.

Compassion shone in Ebony's eyes. "Oh, I'm so sorry, Loretta. George lost his job a few years ago, and we faced a tough financial crisis, too, but the Lord brought us through."

"I'm praying that He will do the same for Edward and me."

Ebony patted Loretta on the arm. "He will, Sweetheart. Don't you worry. He's faithful."

Just then, Cholena Cohanzick entered the room, her long black hair beautifully braided in the tradition of her Lenni Lenape ancestors. "Hello, ladies. Sorry I'm late."

"I'm sorry I'm late, too." Ornella Lombardo, the last of the group, followed closely behind Cholena. "*Ciao, amiche*. Hello, friends." Her face glowed with warmth. Ornella and her family were among the first Italian immigrants to settle in Cape May. She had once told Loretta that she'd chosen the lovely seaside town because it reminded her of her little coastal village in southern Italy.

Once everyone was seated and settled, Clarissa stood. "Let's open with prayer. Heavenly Father, we thank You for this wonderful group of women. Bless our time together as we knit for the needy. And give our sister Loretta Your peace that passes understanding. In the Name of Jesus, we pray."

Loretta's heart warmed as everyone added an *amen* to Clarissa's prayer. These women loved the Lord. Each had her own trials, yet each was ready to help those in need. Loretta was so thankful she could call them her friends and sisters in Christ.

But none of them had faced bankruptcy. Did they really understand how she felt?

Thursday evening, February 20, 1873

As a pale moon rose in the eastern sky, Jeremiah sank into his favorite chair and, with both hands, lifted his limp leg on to the ottoman. Despite his earlier misgivings, the store anniversary celebration two days before had gone well. Several old customers had attended, and several new ones had come as well. He hoped the event would cause business to pick up a bit.

Seemed as though the economy had started to show signs of a decline, including the fishing industry. A decline in the industry meant a decline in the need for fishing supplies. He'd do everything he could to pre-empt future financial problems. If the store didn't succeed, there wasn't much else he could do to earn a living. Because of his bad leg, he couldn't go back to trawler-fishing. So, he had to make a go of it right where he was.

This small room at the back of his store had been his home for the last three years. He would much have preferred to live in the bigger apartment upstairs, but he'd had to rent it out in order to supplement his income. The current tenant would be leaving in April, so he'd have to start looking for a new tenant before then.

He sighed and closed his eyes, the burdens of life threatening to overwhelm him. His mind drifted back to his beloved Anna Mae. When she was alive, he could share his burdens with her, and they became lighter. Anna Mae had been the light of his life. How eagerly they'd awaited their firstborn child after four years of marriage. Jeremiah had planned his fishing trips around her due date, intending to be home for his child's birth. But a premature delivery had disrupted his plans and left him a childless widower.

He blinked back the stinging tears that never failed to rise upon his remembrance of his late wife. What would their lives have been like had she lived? Had their baby boy lived? He would now be seven years old. Jeremiah swallowed hard. He would never know. At least, not on this earth.

He shook his head and lassoed his thoughts. Thinking about something that could never be would only torment him. Perhaps that was the reason the Good

Book instructed him to forget what lay behind and to press forward. Besides, Scripture commanded him to take every thought captive and to lay it at the foot of the Cross.

Press forward. Yes, that's what he must do. But there was a difference between pressing forward and moving forward. The former required courage, strength, persistence. The latter required nothing but a passive drifting along with the flow of life. Which would he choose? The noble way or the cowardly way?

He knew himself. He'd choose the noble way. The courageous way.

The hard way.

Years of trawler fishing had taught him how to handle a storm. You had to confront it head-on. You had to master it before it mastered you. And you had to conquer it with everything you had.

He stretched his legs in front of him. Tom's words about a woman's touch crossed the threshold of his mind again. Jeremiah hadn't even considered such a thing since Anna Mae's death. Was God telling him something?

He dismissed the thought. He barely made enough to take care of himself, let alone a wife. Besides, who would want him? Anna Mae had understood his gruff ways. She'd known how to smooth out his rough edges. Defuse his angry outbursts. Soothe his worrisome ways.

She'd been his perfect complement. Perfect companion. She'd been his heart. Chances of ever finding another woman like her were remote, if not non-existent.

A hard lump formed in his throat. He pushed it down. Better not think about such things. They served no good purpose.

The old clock on the bookshelf struck ten. Time to get some sleep. He needed to rise early in the morning to mend the backyard fence before he opened the shop.

Burrows hopped onto his lap and purred. The cat had belonged to Anna Mae and was the only tangible part of her remaining to him.

He shifted in his chair and cleared his throat. "You startled me, Burrows. You have this strange habit of suddenly appearing out of nowhere. You're enough to make a grown man tremble." Jeremiah curled his fingers in Burrows' neck fur and chuckled.

The cat meowed, yawned, and curled up on his lap.

"Why, thank you. I was just going to get up to go to bed. Have you settled here for the night?"

When Burrows did not budge, Jeremiah looked down at her. She was fast asleep.

"Well, so much for going to bed early. Looks as though I'll be sleeping here for the rest of the night."

Placing his hand on Burrow's thick fur, Jeremiah allowed himself to nod off, strangely comforted by his feline companion.

Saturday, February 22, 1873

The day of Edward's fiftieth birthday party loomed dark and gray, matching the mood in Loretta's heart. She stood in the solarium, ensuring that everything was in order for the celebration. Molly had done an excellent job of setting the tables and arranging a small bouquet of daisies on each one. The room had been festively decorated with colored ribbons, and the large birthday cake had been placed on display in a far corner of the room.

The only element missing was the guest of honor.

Loretta's stomach ached. Thank God for Molly. What would Loretta do without her? She knew how to make the best of the worst situation.

Loretta took in a deep breath. In an hour, she would welcome her first guests. Some of Edward's family would be coming from Tennessee and Oklahoma. Others—friends whom they hadn't seen in years—would arrive from Midwestern and Southern states.

She and Molly had spent the entire previous day preparing the many varieties of food, among them Edward's favorites. But, alas, Edward was on the high seas, on his way to Liverpool, leaving her to clean up the mess he'd so rudely left behind.

Molly entered and curtsied. "Mrs. Vye, the first guests have arrived."

Loretta straightened her shoulders, smoothed the skirt of her dress, and forced herself to put on a smile. "Excellent. Please show them in."

"Yes, ma'am." Molly gave another curtsy and left.

The first to arrive was Edward's brother, Wilbur, and his wife Felicia, all the way from Ohio. "My dear Loretta, how good to see you again." Felicia gave her a warm hug. "We have been awaiting this celebration for a long time."

Loretta returned the hug. "It's good to see you, too, Felicia. And you as well, Wilbur."

Wilbur gave Loretta a heedless kiss on the cheek. "How is that old brother of mine?"

Loretta's muscles tensed. "Well, that old brother of yours is on his way to Liverpool."

Wilbur raised an eyebrow. "What? Surely you're joking."

"I'm afraid not." Heat rose to Loretta's face. "He was called away on urgent business."

Felicia narrowed her eyes. "What kind of urgent business could supersede his fiftieth birthday party?"

Loretta lowered her voice as other guests arrived. "Edward said that if he did not make this trip now, we could lose our entire fortune."

Felicia gasped. "Oh, dear. That is an urgent matter."

Wilbur protested. "Now, now, Felicia." He waved his hand. "You know that Edward always makes things seem worse than they are."

Loretta intervened. "Perhaps so, but this time, Wilbur, I believe that he may have been right in his assessment of the situation."

A group of people approached Loretta. She excused herself. "I'm sorry, but I must attend to the guests who have just arrived. Please help yourselves to some *hors-d'oeuvres* over there on the sideboard."

One by one, Loretta greeted her guests, while Molly directed them to the food beautifully arrayed on the sideboards. The last to arrive were Edward's childhood friend, Jonathan Oberlie and his wife Lucinda, from Salem, Massachusetts.

Lucinda embraced Loretta with a smile. “Hello, dear Loretta. I hope we aren't late.”

“No, no. You're right on time.” She returned Lucinda’s hug.

Jonathan cleared his throat, his bright red bowtie tight against his throat. “So, where is the old chap?”

Blood rushed to Loretta's head. “He's away on business.”

Jonathan's eyes widened. “On business? What business could be more important than one's fiftieth birthday celebration?”

Loretta released a long breath. “I wish you'd been here to ask Edward that very question before he left.”

Jonathan folded his hands across his ample waist. “Well, I'm not completely surprised. Edward was never one to be swayed by anyone. He's always done what he wants to do.”

Indeed. Edward's sensitivities had always leaned toward his business, not toward Loretta—a truth that had caused her great anguish over the years of their marriage.

Lucinda broke in. “But, Jonathan, what an affront to Loretta, don't you think?”

Jonathan cleared his throat. “I'm not here to cast

stones. I'm very sorry I've missed Edward. I haven't seen the old boy in fifteen years." He chuckled. "But I'm not going to let his absence spoil my fun at his birthday party."

Part of Loretta appreciated Jonathan's levity; part of her resented it. "That's certainly a good attitude to adopt."

Lucinda gave Jonathan a sorrowful look. "And to think we made the long trip all the way from Massachusetts and won't get to see him."

Loretta's heart sank. "Oh, I am so sorry, Lucinda. I had no way of contacting you in time. Edward left but two days ago."

Jonathan glared at his wife. "Well, we've gotten to see Loretta, half of this marital equation. And, I might add, the better half. Despite the fact that Edward and I were childhood friends, I've always admonished him about his tendency toward selfishness." Jonathan patted Loretta's hand. "No need to worry, my dear. We shall make the best of things. And I advise you to do the same. When I next catch up with that old codger, I will give him a piece of my mind."

Lucinda sighed. "A big piece, I hope."

Chapter Three

Monday, March 3, 1873

Monday mornings at Jeremiah's Fishing Supply Store were always busy as fishermen prepared for another week of work on the high seas. Jeremiah rose especially early this Monday morning to receive the supply wagons that would be coming in from the harbor. But first, he'd have his coffee.

Burrows stood at his feet, her eyes begging for her breakfast. He looked down at her and laughed. "Would you kindly give a man a moment to finish his coffee?"

She sidled up to his shin and rubbed her soft fur against it.

"That's a good girl." He reached into the cupboard

and pulled out some scraps left over from dinner. Burrows followed at his heels as Jeremiah poured the scraps into her bowl. She pounced on the food before he'd finished pouring it. "My, my. I've never seen you so hungry."

She devoured the meal within two minutes. Then, licking her lips, she retired to the sun-splashed windowsill in the front part of the store where she immediately settled in for a nap.

"Well, if that isn't the good life, I don't know what is." Jeremiah stood watching her for a long moment. Anna Mae used to love sitting in the sunshine, too, with Burrows on her lap. How he missed his precious wife! It seemed as though the older he got, the lonelier he felt. In recent days, the thought of growing old all alone had begun to bother him. Was it that he was approaching the half-century mark of his life? Or did the quieter pace of life on land give him more time to think?

The bell above the front door tinkled. Sam Strittmatter walked in, a big smile on his face. "Good mornin' to you, Jeremiah."

"Why, good morning, Sam! What can I do for you today?"

"I'm needin' some flounder bait. It's such a beautiful day, I thought I'd go catch me some flounder on the bay and fry it up real good for dinner tonight."

"Sounds delicious!" Jeremiah walked over to an upper shelf and located the flounder bait. "Here you go, Sam. That'll be a half dollar."

Sam paid him and then lingered a moment. "I found myself a good woman, Jeremiah. I wanted you to be among the first to know."

"Why, that's wonderful, Sam. A good woman is hard to find these days."

Sam grinned. "We'll be gettin' married in July. Sure would like you to come to the weddin'."

Jeremiah's heart warmed. "It would be an honor, Sam. Thank you for thinking of me."

Sam's face grew red. "Sure thing. You've been a good friend to me ever since I moved to Cape May. I'm much indebted to for your wisdom and counsel during a few rough spots in my life."

"We all have them, Sam. Rough spots that is. But with the Lord at our side, we make it through everyone." He grew pensive. "Remember that especially in your marriage."

"Will do. Thank you, Jeremiah." He smiled. 'Well, I'd better be gettin' to the bay before all the flounder get caught."

As Sam exited the store, Jeremiah called out. "The

early bird catches the worm." He laughed. "Or should I say, the *flounder*?"

Monday, March 3, 1873

Loretta sat at the kitchen table, wringing her hands as she waited for Molly to come down. It had been four days since Edward's scheduled arrival in Liverpool, and she still had not heard from him. He'd promised to send her a telegram upon his arrival. What could possibly be the cause for his delay? He knew how she fretted over such things. Had he no compassion for her feelings?

Molly walked into the room. "Good mornin' to you, Mrs. Vye."

Loretta smiled. "Good morning, Molly."

"Is somethin' troublin' you, ma'am?"

"Yes. Four days have elapsed since Edward's arrival in Liverpool, and I have yet to hear from him."

No sooner had Loretta spoken the words than there was a knock at the door.

Molly opened the door to find the telegram delivery boy standing outside.

"This is for Mrs. Vye, ma'am. Be so kind as to give it to her, please."

Molly took the telegram from him. "Yes, I will. Do you need a signature?"

"No, ma'am. I don't." He tipped his hat. "Top o' the mornin' to you."

Molly closed the door and then handed the telegram to Loretta. "This may be what you've been waitin' for, ma'am."

Loretta's muscles tensed as she took the telegram from Molly. "Thank you." She rose and went to the sitting room. Her hands shook as she tore open the seal to read the telegram. It was from Edward.

My Dearest Loretta,

I trust that you are well. I am sending you this missive to inform you that I will need to remain a few extra days in London. I had hoped to have rejoined you sooner, but I must attend to this matter before I embark on my return trip. I trust you will understand.

Your devoted husband,

Edward

. . .

Her blood temperature skyrocketed to boiling point. She crushed the telegram in the palm of her hand and tossed it on the floor next to her. Edward always expected understanding *from* her but rarely had any *for* her. This was the story of her life. Edward's frequent trips. His repeated delays. His myriad excuses for his never-ending absences. All because of financial problems with his business.

She rubbed her temples with her fingers in a futile attempt to ease the headache that hammered her more frequently of late. What choice did she have but to trust him? He knew more than she about financial matters. He was the provider. The decision-maker. Yet at times she wished he would give her more details about what was truly going on. Not knowing was worse than knowing the worst. She could handle the worst. But she found it extremely difficult to handle the unknown.

She was only a woman after all. What did she know about financial matters? She had no competence in that area. Besides, contrary to her dear Molly's assertions, women were meant to follow, not to lead.

Yet that very concept needled her, got under her skin, irritated her very sense of justice. Were women created only to be mere puppets of men? Surely a woman had more common sense than a man. Moreover, while physically stronger than women, men were certainly the weaker sex when it came to morality.

Her mind drifted back to her own mother. As much as Mama loved Papa, she'd often warned Loretta never to trust a man for her financial well-being. When a woman lost her financial independence, she lost everything.

Mama had been right. But living with Aunt Martha had overshadowed much of Mama's wise counsel and had replaced it with a steady dose of criticism and condescension toward Loretta.

She was growing tired of living the life of a married widow. She would express her displeasure to Edward upon his return.

Meanwhile, she'd have another chat with Molly about—what had Molly called it?—the "lie of the century." The belief that a true woman was a totally submissive one—one concerned only with her home and her family. The belief that for a woman to reach beyond the confines of the home was to over-reach.

The more Loretta thought about it, the more Molly seemed right. Loretta would find out more from the young woman she loved as a daughter. And, if what she learned from Molly proved to be true, Loretta would have more than a little changing to do.

* * *

Tuesday, March 4, 1873, 2:30 pm

At the sound of knocking on the back door, Loretta looked up from her copy of *Middlemarch* by George Eliot. She'd buried herself in the novel's pages to escape her painful loneliness while waiting for Molly to return from her lunch break. The girl had gone to fetch her beau and bring him to meet her mistress.

Loretta rose to answer the door. There before her stood a beaming Molly with a very handsome young man at her side.

Loretta smiled broadly. "Do come in!" Enthusiasm filled her voice.

A lovely blush on her face, Molly entered first and then turned to the young man following close behind her. "Mrs. Vye, I'd like to introduce you to my beau, Sean O'Leary. Sean, this is Mrs. Loretta Vye, my mistress."

Loretta extended her right hand. "I am so pleased to meet you, Mr. O'Leary."

The young man lowered his eyes. "Sean, please, ma'am. Please call me Sean."

Loretta nodded. "I've heard such wonderful things about you, Sean."

This time it was Sean who blushed. "And I about you, Mrs. Vye."

Loretta motioned them to the sitting room. "Please. Come sit down. May I get you a cup of tea?"

Molly shook her head. "No, thank you, Mrs. Vye. Sean and I just finished our lunch."

"Then please sit down."

Molly took a place on the sofa across from Loretta's chair. Sean sat down beside her.

Loretta returned to her reading chair. "I have been looking forward to this visit ever since Molly first told me about you."

Sean fingered the cap in his hand. "I must confess, ma'am, that I'm a bit nervous."

Loretta chuckled. "Well, I would be, too, if I were in your shoes. I suppose Molly has told you that any young man in whom she is interested must first pass my approval."

"Yes, ma'am." He glanced at Molly. "Molly informed me as much."

A lump formed in Loretta's throat. "Although I have no children of my own, Molly has become the daughter I never had. So, I am very cautious about protecting her."

"As well you should be, ma'am." Sean placed his cap beside him.

"So, tell me a little about yourself, Sean."

"I be from Ireland, ma'am, from the same village as Molly. But we didn't know each other until after comin' to America." Sean gave Molly a sheepish smile . "We met at church, in fact. Molly's angelic voice in the choir sparked somethin' in my heart."

Loretta loved the young man's open sincerity. "Indeed. Molly has an angelic voice. She often sings around here while doing chores."

"Then you know exactly what I mean, ma'am." Sean grinned.

"Indeed, I do."

Molly's face radiated at the praise of her beau.

Sean's eyes were glued to her. "I work at the livery stable on the edge of town. Since boyhood, horses have always fascinated me, so I decided to make shoein' them my trade."

"And a good trade it is, Sean. Shoeing horses is a regular need."

"Yes, ma'am." He smiled. "That was my thinkin' too."

Molly shifted to the edge of her seat and folded her hands on her lap. Her face glowed. "Mrs. Vye, Sean and I are going to be married."

The exuberance in her voice warmed Loretta's heart. She leaned forward. "Well, that is wonderful news! When is the big day?"

"This coming Saturday, ma'am." Molly glanced at Sean. "And we'd like to invite you to the weddin'."

"Why, I would be delighted to attend." Loretta sighed. "I am sorry that Edward will not be here to share in your celebration. He is due back from England the following week."

"Should we be waitin', then, ma'am?"

"Oh, by no means, dear child! You must make your own plans." Loretta hesitated and lowered her voice. "Just as Edward made his." She stifled the bitter taste that lately rose more frequently from her stomach. She hastened to change the subject. "Do you need any help with the wedding?"

"No ma'am. I already have me weddin' dress, and our pastor has graciously offered a meetin' room at our church for the reception."

"That's such a blessing."

"A blessin' it is, ma'am." Molly squeezed Sean's hand. "Well, ma'am, we won't be takin' any more of your time. I'll be gettin' back to work upstairs, and Sean will be returnin' to the livery."

Loretta's heart melted at the visible love between the young couple before her. She rose. "Sean, it was a blessing to meet you." She looked him squarely in the eye. "Take good care of my Molly, do you hear me?" Her voice was firm but loving. "She is a treasure."

Sean looked at Molly. "That I know for sure, ma'am."

Loretta's gaze followed them as Molly accompanied Sean to the door. Loretta whispered a prayer that God would protect their love and that it would grow even deeper from year to year.

Just as her love for Edward and his for her had grown over their nineteen years of marriage.

But would their love continue to grow if he brought back unsettling news about their finances?

Chapter Four

Tuesday, March 4, 1873

"I was quite impressed with your husband-to-be." Loretta gave Molly a warm smile after Sean had left. "He is a humble man with a good heart. He will love you well."

Molly blushed as she held up the teapot. "Thank you, ma'am. Sean was quite impressed with you as well. He said you are a very kind woman, and he's right."

Loretta's heart warmed. "Any kindness I come by, dear Molly, is only by the grace of God. I can be quite the contrary and dispirited woman under the right circumstances."

Molly poured hot water into Loretta's cup.

Loretta steadied the cup. "So you must be quite excited."

"I'm jumpin' on the inside."

Loretta laughed. Oh, the joy of young love!

Molly drew in a deep breath. "I can't adequately be espressin' me excitement, Mrs. Vye. 'Tis beyond words."

"I understand." But did she really? Loretta's marriage with Edward had been arranged by her Uncle Malcolm at the insistence of her hateful Aunt Martha. Not that Loretta hadn't wanted to be free of that awful woman. She'd stuffed Loretta into a cage of impossible rules and awful punishments for breaking them. Anything to make her niece long for the nearest way of escape.

That way had been Edward, although theirs was a relationship of mutual understanding and companionship, not the passionate love she'd hoped for in a marriage. The kind of love for a man now reflected in Molly's eyes.

Loretta sighed. She would never know that kind of love. Edward was a matter-of-fact person. He handled his marriage the same way he handled his business—in a calm, cool, and collected manner. *Pragmatist* would be the best word to describe him. Certainly not *romantic*. Why, it did not even seem to bother him that he'd miss his own birthday party.

Loretta lassoed her straying thoughts. "I am so excited for you, Molly. I have just the dress I can wear to your wedding. Would you like to see it?"

Molly's eyes widened. "Oh, yes, Mrs. Vye. I would."

"Come with me, then." Loretta led the way to her bedroom where she opened the large mahogany armoire, a bequest from Edward's mother upon her death several years earlier. She opened the double doors and pulled out a lovely linen sky-blue dress, decorated with little pearls around the neckline. "Do you like it?"

"Oh, Mrs. Vye. It will look stunning on you, especially with your blue eyes."

"I wanted something comfortable, yet suitable for an occasion as important as your wedding. Does it pass your inspection?"

Molly laughed. "Dear me, Mrs. Vye, it needn't pass my inspection, only yours."

Loretta took Molly gently by the shoulders. "You have no idea how happy I am for you, my dear Molly." Tears welled up in her eyes. "I don't know what I would have done without you all these years." She smiled through her tears. "And now, to see you soon to be married gives me a joy I simply cannot contain."

Molly's eyes glistened. "I be much beholdin' to you, Mrs. Vye. I don't know what I would have done without you either. You believed in me enough to employ me when I had no family or friends. If it weren't for your kindness, I don't know where I'd be. Probably back in Ireland."

"I'm glad I have been of some help to you." Loretta cleared her throat. "And now, let's go have ourselves a cup of tea. I baked some apple scones to go with them."

After a brief break for tea and scones, Loretta retired to her bedroom where, once again, she picked up her knitting. The repeated knit-purl motion helped distract her from her emptiness. When Edward returned, she'd stir the passion in her marriage. Perhaps her relationship with Edward could become more like that between Molly and Sean.

Saturday, March 8, 1873

The day of Molly's wedding soon arrived. Loretta dressed carefully in front of her tall, standing mirror. If only Edward were here to attend the ceremony with her. Over the years of their married life, his business had kept him from participating in many social events with her. Attending alone was awkward, but she'd gone, nonetheless, to pay her respects and not wanting to miss out on much-needed human companionship because of Edward's absence. She sighed.

A pang of guilt coursed through her. She shouldn't focus on the negative. Edward was working hard for her to secure her financial future. Shouldn't she be grateful? He had, after all, sent her a telegram stating that he'd arrived safely in Liverpool and would need to spend a few more days in London before his return voyage, scheduled to depart on Thursday, March twentieth and to arrive in New York on Tuesday, April first. She'd circled the date on her calendar, anticipating special things she'd do for him upon his return. Perhaps he would no longer want to travel as much when he realized how pleasant it was to be in his own home with the woman he loved.

She stared into the mirror. She'd have to do her hair by herself today since Molly, who usually did it for her, was preparing for her wedding.

A sweep of the brush, a lifting of the long blond tresses, and a pinning here and there sufficed. Not that anyone would care about her hairstyle. Perhaps

Edward would comment on it if he were here. More likely, he would not.

Would he return with good news or bad? If only Loretta knew what was going on. Not knowing kept her tossing and turning at night, imagining the worst. Why didn't Edward confide in her about their financial situation? Did he think her unable to understand? Did he view her as incompetent, the way Aunt Martha had viewed her? Her aunt had frequently expressed disdain at what she viewed as Loretta's lack of intellect. *Stupidity*, Aunt Martha would call it. Every time she spoke the word, it pierced Loretta's soul, to the point she'd started to believe it.

But no. She wasn't stupid. Only uninformed. Her mind drifted back to the days of her early childhood. Papa would call her brilliant, and Mama would call her beautiful.

Aunt Martha called her neither.

The sharp talons of her aunt's unkind words on Loretta's impressionable, young heart still dug deep into her soul. No matter how much she tried to disengage herself from them, she could not escape their tight grip. To this day, when facing a new challenge, Loretta would hear her aunt's disparaging comments: *You can't do that, Loretta. You're too stupid.*

Loretta dodged the fiery mental darts and glanced

at the clock on the mantel. She had a half hour to get to the church before the wedding ceremony at eleven o'clock. Grabbing her woolen cloak from the bed where she'd laid it, she placed it over her shoulders and left her bedroom. She picked up her reticule from the hall table, locked the door behind her, and left.

The day was cold and brisk, but sunny. A good day for a wedding. Loretta whispered a prayer for Molly and Sean. As she approached the church, a small group of people entered. Loretta followed close behind and was approached by a young man with a broad smile on his face.

"Hello. I'm Sean's cousin. Robert."

"I'm Loretta Vye, Molly's employer. I am pleased to meet you, Robert."

"Likewise, ma'am. May I show you to your seat?'

Loretta smiled as she took his offered arm. "Yes, of course."

She followed him down the aisle to the front pew. She was the last one to be seated, at the end of the pew. Wonderful. She'd have a good view of Molly walking down the aisle.

The organist intoned the first note of Pachelbel's *Canon in D Major* and everyone stood. First came one female attendant, followed by one male attendant.

Then appeared Molly, regaled as a queen and escorted by an elder from her church.

Molly's face beamed with joy as her gaze locked on to her beloved's. Tears welled up in Loretta's eyes as she remembered her own wedding day. Would that Edward were here to witness the ceremony! But then again, Edward was not the romantic she was. He would have considered it but a pleasant distraction from the routine of daily life. A routine that always involved his business.

A pang of guilt assailed Loretta's conscience. She chided herself. If there were anything she hated, it was ingratitude.

She heaved a deep sigh and shifted her attention to Molly and Sean at the altar as they exchanged their solemn vows. The sweet fragrance of lilies filled the sanctuary while a lark on the maple tree just outside the window sang its melodious song.

Soon the minister pronounced Molly and Sean man and wife. When the young couple turned to face the congregation, the tears in Loretta's eyes streamed down her cheeks. Molly was radiant, and Sean beamed with delight. Theirs truly was a marriage made in heaven.

Loretta swallowed the lump in her throat. Would that hers had been as well.

* * *

Tuesday, April 1, 1873

Loretta sat in the large blue wing chair in her bedroom, her latest knitting project resting untouched on her lap. Thank God for her knitting. Having been taught how to knit by her mother, Loretta considered it the one thing in which she excelled. As a young girl, she would spend hours knitting while hiding in her bedroom to avoid Aunt Martha's cruel verbal barbs. Between knitting and reading, she'd managed to shield herself to some extent from her aunt's relentless criticism and condescension.

Now knitting helped her fill the long, lonely hours while Edward was away. What good was it being married when one's spouse was rarely home? One married for companionship, but when that companionship was lacking, the marriage suffered.

She drew in a deep breath and picked up her latest project, a brightly colored scarf for an orphaned child. The sunlight played on the vibrant colors, dancing off each one as though excited about the child's future reaction to the gift. Loretta's imagination blossomed as she pictured it. Perhaps the bright colors would brighten the child's heart.

The sunset was lovely through the nearby window that overlooked the back lawn. The maple trees were in full blossom now, and through the open window, the first bird songs of spring carried. April had arrived, and with it, Edward's imminent return to Cape May.

At that very moment, he was aboard the *SS Atlantic* on its return trip from Liverpool to New York. In one more day, on Thursday, April third, the ship would dock in New York Harbor. From there, Edward would take a train to Philadelphia and then a carriage to Cape May. So had he written in the letter he'd dispatched immediately prior to his sailing from Liverpool on Thursday, March twentieth.

Loretta sighed. She would be glad to have him home again. There was only so much cleaning and rearranging of furniture that a woman could do before lapsing into boredom.

A loud rap on her door startled her from her thoughts. "Come in."

Molly burst through the door, a look of concern on her face. "Mrs. Vye, the telegram boy just delivered this telegram for you. He said it was urgent."

Loretta's heart leapt to her throat. She took the telegram from Molly's extended hand and read *White*

Star Line on the envelope. Her body froze. The *SS Atlantic* was one of the ships belonging to *White Star*.

Her hands trembled as she opened the telegram and read: *SS Atlantic shipwrecked off coast of Nova Scotia. Edward Vye not listed among survivors. Sincere regrets and condolences. Contact steamship line for details.*

Loretta's heart stopped as a wail rose to her throat and lodged there. She grabbed the gold cross around her neck. Her limbs grew numb. The room around her spun as she struggled to breathe. The telegram slipped from her hand and dropped to the floor.

"What is it, ma'am?" Molly stooped to pick it up and fanned Loretta with it. "Mrs. Vye. Are you all right?" Molly handed the telegram back to her.

Loretta laid aside her knitting and rose slowly, still holding the telegram. "It's Edward. His ship was wrecked yesterday." She fell forward, barely catching the fireplace mantel to support herself. "He's dead."

Molly gasped. "O God in heav'n, have mercy!" She reached for Loretta. "Please. Sit down, Mrs. Vye." She helped Loretta back into her chair.

Loretta rested her head on the back of the chair, unable to speak. This couldn't be true. Surely Edward was one of the survivors. Surely he would be home in two days as planned. Surely it was all a bad dream.

Her emotions drifted in and out of hope and despair. Only the repeated patting of Molly's hand on hers signaled to Loretta that she was still alive.

"Mrs. Vye! Mrs. Vye! I'm going to fetch Doctor Higgins."

Loretta could only nod. Old Doc Higgins lived at the far end of the street, a two-minute walk from Loretta's house. Perhaps he would give her something to calm her nerves. She needed to be able to think clearly.

Molly knelt by her side. "I'll be back shortly. Promise me you won't move."

"I promise." Loretta forced out the words.

While Molly was gone, Loretta read the telegram again. The words blurred through her tears. *Shipwrecked. Not among survivors.* She shook her head. No. Edward was not dead. Edward could not be dead. There had to be some mistake.

Molly returned in short order with Dr. Higgins following close behind. He placed his leather bag on the floor and pulled up a chair beside Loretta. "Now, then, I hear you've had some alarming news."

Loretta nodded. "Yes." Her reply was barely a whisper.

Doc Higgins took her wrist to check her pulse. "I'm going to give you something to calm your nerves.

Then, I'm going to pray with you for wisdom as to what to do next."

Thank goodness for the doctor's help and especially for his prayers. She needed the Lord's wisdom now more than ever. But would He give it, after she'd neglected Him for so long? After she'd doubted Him for so long?

Doc Higgins retrieved a small vial of laudanum from his leather bag. He turned toward Molly. "I want you to give her one-half teaspoon of this in the morning and in the evening. Do this for three days."

Molly nodded emphatically. "Yes, Doctor."

After praying with Loretta, Doc Higgins rose to leave. "I want you to rest now, Loretta, do you hear me? There will be time enough in the days ahead to make necessary decisions."

Loretta nodded again and closed her eyes. Decisions. Yes, many decisions. Difficult decisions. But was she capable of making those decisions? Edward had taken care of everything. What would she do without him? Would she be able to survive? To overcome? To take care of herself? She had wanted her chance, but not like this. Oh, not like this.

Her heart heavy with grief, she drifted into unsettled sleep.

Chapter Five

Tuesday, April 1, 1873

Jeremiah prayed a silent prayer of thanks as several customers browsed his store. Despite the decline in the general economy, it seemed his fears about the effect on his business had been premature. People still needed to eat, and that meant fishing. If his business continued to grow like this, he'd soon have to hire someone to help him. Not that he minded. A growing business was a good thing. A blessing from the Lord. Especially in a difficult economy.

"Good morning, Sam." Jeremiah greeted Sam Strittmatter. "What can I do for you today?"

"The same thing you do every time I come." He

chuckled. “Ring up my sale.” Although gruff in his ways, Sam had a good heart. He reminded Jeremiah of Nathaniel, a man in whom Jesus said there was no guile.

“Much obliged to you, Sam. You've been a faithful customer ever since I first opened my store.”

“And a satisfied one. You've done right by me, Jeremiah.”

“That's my aim.”

Sam handed Jeremiah his payment for the fishing tackle he'd purchased. “So have you heard about the shipwreck off the coast of Nova Scotia?”

Jeremiah's muscles tensed. “No. I haven't. What happened?”

“Seems like the *SS Atlantic* sank after hitting rocks off the coast of Meagher's Island, west of Halifax, during a storm in the middle of the night. It was on its way back from Liverpool. Several hundred people drowned at sea.”

Jeremiah shook his head, an ache overtaking his heart. “How tragic! So sorry to hear this.” He’d fished off the coast of Nova Scotia and knew of the treacherous rocks in that area. He'd also seen a few shipwrecks in his day, and none of them had been pretty. The worst part was the suffering of the families left behind.

But what of the lighthouse in Halifax Harbor? Had the ship's captain not seen it? Something must have gone wrong.

Sam cleared his throat. "I'm sure we'll be hearing more once the newspapers are printed." He retrieved his change from Jeremiah. "Thank you."

"You're welcome, Sam."

Sam's news left Jeremiah with a troubling ache in his heart. Any death reminded him of Anna Mae. He grieved for those who would soon receive news that their loved one had died in that shipwreck. He understood the feeling of helplessness that would accompany that news, and his heart broke for those on the receiving end of it.

He drew in a deep breath. Why did he take on the pain of others as he did? Did one's own suffering make one more sensitive to the suffering of others? It seemed so.

Burrows jumped onto the counter and purred. Jeremiah rubbed her back. Did animals sense the pain of humans? The dear cat nudged her head under Jeremiah's palm. He gave her a head rub and then returned to his work.

As the day progressed, other customers shared the news of the disastrous shipwreck. By nightfall, it had become the main topic of conversation among the residents of Cape May. What could he do to help?

Tuesday, April 1, 1873

It was night when Loretta awakened. A strong wind beat against the shutters, moaning like an injured child. Loretta threw off the covers and sat upright in bed, trying to get her bearings.

The telegram from the steamship company floated to her remembrance. Grabbing her robe from the foot of the bed, she donned it and hurried to her desk. The telegram lay there, just where she'd left it earlier that day. The temptation to reread it wrestled with her desire never to look at it again.

The temptation won.

Loretta lit the oil lamp, picked up the wrinkled piece of paper and read again the painful words. She shook her head. Impossible. In two days, Edward would walk through the front door, put down his travel bag, and sweep her into his arms. She would hold him close, ask about his trip, and all would be well.

A sob clutched at her throat. The telegram lay in

her hands, wet with her tears. She crumpled it and let it fall to the floor. She would contact the steamship company for details about Edward's death, if for no other reason than to feel as though she were doing something to relieve the unbearable ache in her heart.

She opened the desk drawer and took out a piece of writing paper, a small bottle of ink, and her quill pen. She placed all three on the desk and wrote quickly.

Please send details on passenger Edward Vye involved in SS Atlantic *wreckage.*

Sincerely,

His devoted wife,
Loretta Vye

She could not bring herself to write the word *deceased*. It was so painful. So hopeless. So final.

As soon as Molly arrived in the morning, Loretta would have her take the message to the telegraph office. She had to know how the wreck had occurred and how

Edward had died. She could not go on living in this tortuous limbo of uncertainty.

A chill swept over her. She rose and wrapped her robe more tightly around her trembling shoulders. Wringing her hands, she paced her bedroom. What would she do without Edward? How would she survive? How would she manage? All her life, she'd been under someone's care. First, that of her parents. Then, that of Uncle Malcolm and Aunt Martha, despite the harshness of that care. And, finally, that of her husband. She'd never been on her own before. She didn't even know where to start.

The big question was, would she have enough finances to survive? Edward had stated that they might be on the verge of a financial disaster. Had that proven to be the case? His entire reason for going to England had been to ensure that their finances were in order. Had he succeeded in his mission?

Loretta shuffled to the window. The sky was pitch black, like the color of her soul. Darkness outside and inside. And no light in sight.

Waves of panic surged through her. Would the finances be sufficient to sustain her for the rest of her life?

And then there was the most important element—Edward's absence. His protection. His love. She needed his stability, his dry sense of humor, his strength. They were the anchor of her soul. The rock on which she leaned. The reason for which she lived.

She heaved a deep sigh and fell crosswise onto the bed. The silence of the night screamed at her soul, searing it with excruciating pain. Any hope of relief left her. Rising from the depths of her broken heart, heaving sobs wrenched her body and escaped her lips.

She finally yielded her pain to the numbness of sleep.

* * *

Wednesday, April 2, 1873

When Loretta awakened the next morning, the sun had already begun its upward arc. A waning moon appeared through the crack in her lace curtains, announcing its soon departure to give place to the sun.

She rubbed her eyes, swollen from intervals of weeping during the night. Had Molly still been with her at night, she'd have awakened her. But, after Molly's marriage, Loretta had insisted that the dear girl rightfully belonged at her new husband's side.

Molly had not needed much convincing.

Loretta lay in bed for a long while. How she longed to hear Edward's snoring once again. Sense his weight on his side of the bed. Feel the hairs on his arm as she rubbed it while he slept.

She rose, threw off the coverlet, and sat on the edge of the mattress. Horrific images of Edward's drowning at sea assaulted her mind. She shook her head to rid herself of them, but the relentless onslaught grew worse.

She grabbed her robe at the foot of the bed, stood up, and wrapped it tightly around her. Perhaps a cup of hot coffee would clear her head. She made her way down the stairs to the kitchen. Except for the sound of robins on the maple tree outside the back door, the neighborhood was still quiet this time of day. As she prepared the coffee, old Doc Higgins approached the back door.

Loretta opened it before he could knock."Good morning, Doc."

He gave her a warm smile. "Good morning. I see you beat me to it."

"Yes." She opened the door all the way to let him in. "I just got up. Couldn't sleep."

He entered the house and placed his bag on the kitchen table. "I wanted to stop by before I start my office hours. Have you been taking the medicine I gave you?"

Loretta rubbed her forehead. "Molly gave me a dose last night before she left, but I haven't taken anything this morning." She looked around absentmindedly. "In fact, I don't even know where it is. " She sighed. "But Molly will be here soon. I'm sure she put it in a safe place."

Just then, Molly walked through the kitchen door, almost knocking it into the good doctor. "Oh, good mornin', Doctor. So sorry. I didn't see you standin' behind the door."

Doc Higgins quickly stepped aside. "You're just the person I want to see."

Molly raised a questioning eyebrow.

"Where did you put Mrs. Vye's medication?"

Molly pointed to a cupboard to the right of the sink. "It's in there. I'll get it right away." She removed her cloak, set it on the back of a kitchen chair, and retrieved the medication from the cupboard. "Here you go, Doc." She handed the bottle to the doctor.

"Now, Loretta. Be sure to take your medicine for the next three days. It will help to calm your nerves and give you some much-needed sleep."

Loretta nodded, her mind in a fog.

Doc Higgins placed a hand on her shoulder.

"Now, listen to me, Loretta. There's nothing we can do about Edward except pray that the Lord will comfort you in your grief. Meanwhile, I want you strong to face whatever lies ahead."

The man's words landed as an ominous dictum on Loretta's heart. Did he know something she didn't know? Had he heard about Edward's financial situation? Was Doc Higgins trying to protect her from another shocking revelation?

Loretta swallowed hard, unable to find words to respond.

The good doctor cleared his throat. "Very well, then. I must be going." He looked at Molly. "If there is any change for the worse, fetch me at once. I will be in my office until six this evening and at home afterward."

"Yes, Doctor."

He picked up his bag. "No need to show me to the door. You tend to Mrs. Vye." He tilted his head toward Loretta.

Molly nodded.

After Doc Higgins left, Loretta picked up the note she'd written and turned to Molly. "Molly, please take this to the telegraph office immediately."

"But, ma'am, Doc Higgins said—"

Loretta cut her off. "I know what he said. But I also need you to send this telegram to the steamship company. I must know the particulars about Edward's death." She handed Molly the written note.

The girl hesitated. "Very well, ma'am."

Loretta rose slowly, holding on to the edge of the kitchen table.

Molly wrapped an arm around her waist and led her to the sitting room. After settling Loretta in her favorite chair, Molly knelt down in front of her. "Mrs. Vye, you must promise me that you will remain in this chair until I return. I will be back as quickly as I can."

Loretta's voice was barely a whisper. "I promise."

Loretta's gaze followed Molly out the door. Then she leaned her head against the back of the chair. From her throat, a guttural moan rose to her lips. Hot tears buried by restraint finally gushed out in torrential force. "Edward! Oh, Edward! Why did you have to leave me?"

She covered her wail with her handkerchief. But the small piece of cloth could not contain her grief.

Chapter Six

Wednesday, April 2, 1873

Jeremiah spread the morning edition of the *Star of the Cape* newspaper on the counter. In a half hour, he would open the store, but first, he needed to catch up on the news about the shipwreck.

The front page lay before him, with a lithograph of the sunken vessel. His years at sea had taught him that wrecks happened, but that fact never diminished their tragic, sorrowful consequences.

According to the article, the captain of the *SS Atlantic*, James Williams, fearing his fuel supply would run short and that his ship would not make it to New York, had diverted to Halifax to refuel. Never having been to Halifax Harbor, Williams was unaware that the strong currents of the area had driven his ship to the rocky shores of Lower Prospect, a tiny fishing village about twelve miles to the west. The ship crashed full speed into the rocks, splitting apart, and resulting in the death of several hundred people. The newspaper called it the largest sea disaster in the North Atlantic up to that time.

Jeremiah shook his head and sighed. He whispered a prayer for the families of the deceased.

A sharp knock on the front door interrupted his reading. Jeremiah opened it to find Tom Brogan waiting on the other side. "What are you doing up so early?"

Tom smiled. "Thought you'd like to chew the fat over a cup of coffee before you open the store."

"Sounds good." Jeremiah stood aside to admit his friend, then shut and locked the door behind him. "Coffee's already brewing."

Tom took a seat at the table. In a few moments, Jeremiah placed two steaming mugs on the table.

Burrows jumped onto Tom's lap, but he scooted her away. "Hey, cat! Don't you go jumpin' all over me. You know how I feel about cats."

Jeremiah laughed. "Burrows likes you."

"Well, I don't like her. I'm not partial to any animal."

"I love dogs myself." Jeremiah sighed. "But this was Anna Mae's cat. It's my only remaining physical connection to her."

Tom grew serious. "Sorry, buddy. I didn't know that, or I never would have shooed the poor creature away." He leaned over. "Come on over here, Burrows. Uncle Tom wants to ask your forgiveness."

Touched by his friend's gesture, Jeremiah scooped up the insulted cat and handed her to Tom. "Here. Now make your amends."

Burrows hunched her back and raised her claws toward Tom.

Tom backed off. "Whoa, girl!" He recoiled, hands in the air. "Just like a woman. There's no end to her vengeance when she's been burnt."

Jeremiah took back his cat. "Sounds as though you haven't had any good relationships with women."

Tom grew wistful. "Had meself one once." His eyes misted over. "But that was many moons ago." He glanced at Jeremiah. "When I was a young whipper-snapper with no common sense."

Jeremiah saw right through his friend's façade of bravado. "Have you ever thought of getting married?"

Tom guffawed. "Who, me? You gotta be kiddin'. I ain't the marryin' type." He paused. "Although I can't deny if the right woman came along, I might consider it."

"What do you mean by the right woman?"

"She's gotta be perty, tough, and a good cook."

"Tough?"

"Yeah. To put up with an old curmudgeon like me."

Jeremiah laughed and then sobered. "Did you hear about the shipwreck up by Nova Scotia yesterday?"

"Yeah, heard about it late last night. The news has been all over town." Tom took a sip of coffee. "Got wind that a local woman lost her husband on that ship."

Jeremiah's ears perked as a pang pierced his gut. "Is that so?"

"Yeah. The man's name was Vye. Edward Vye."

Jeremiah shook his head. "Never heard of him."

"He was some sort of businessman. Somethin' to do with the railroad, I think."

"Too bad. I'm sorry for his widow."

Tom gulped down the rest of his coffee and slapped his hand on the table. "Well, I gotta be gettin' to work." He rose. "If ya ain't got nothin' to do tonight, maybe we could have ourselves a game of checkers."

Jeremiah nodded. "Sounds good. Be here at seven." He chuckled. "And be prepared to lose."

Tom huffed. "Lose? Don't you know you'll be playin' against the winner of the 1873 Checkers Championship of Cape May County?"

Jeremiah snorted. "Since when?"

"Since right now."

Jeremiah placed a hand on Tom's shoulder and smiled. "You may be good at checkers, my friend, but one thing you're not good at is lying."

"You got that right. My mama used to tell me the same thing." He smiled. "See you tonight."

Jeremiah walked to the door with Tom and unlocked it. "Time to open up."

"Hope you do some good business today, me friend."

"I hope so, too."

But for some strange reason, as the morning unfolded, Jeremiah couldn't get that poor widow who'd just lost her husband—what was her name? Mrs. Vye?—off his mind.

Thursday, April 3, 1873

. . .

Her body rigid in the straight-backed, wooden chair, Loretta settled in the attorney's office for the reading of Edward's will. She'd received an urgent summons to meet with him.

The office was small and stuffy, the kind marked by acrid cigar smoke and musty old furniture. In the far corner, a wilting plant stood sentinel, its brown-tinged leaves limp under a narrow, high-ceilinged window through which a shadowed sun cast its long and dust-filled rays.

In front of Loretta stood a massive mahogany desk, with several piles of papers neatly arranged atop it. A green banker's lamp stood on one corner of the desk while a thick tome titled *Encyclopedia of the Law* rested on the other.

Behind the desk sat Mr. Hosea Lamkin, Cape May's only attorney and, thus, Edward's as well. A graying, middle-aged man of robust proportion, sporting a well-trimmed salt-and-pepper beard, Lamkin was of sober demeanor but genteel heart. Known for his expertise in handling estate matters, he was also respected for his genuine care for the welfare of his clients.

"Good morning, Mrs. Vye." Mr. Lamkin gave her a smile and a welcoming nod.

"Good morning, Mr. Lamkin."

He leaned forward, compassion in his eyes. "I know how difficult it is to lose a loved one, so I want to make this as painless as possible for you."

Loretta took in a deep breath. If she hurt any more, she would disintegrate. "Thank you." For the past two days, ever since she'd learned of Edward's death at sea, she'd dreaded this moment. It would mark the discovery of the truth about her financial situation and very likely the turning point for her future survival.

If she did survive.

Her deceased mother's words rose from the depths of Loretta's heart. "You're a champion, Loretta. You can do all things through Christ who gives you strength."

Mama never lied. So why didn't Loretta feel like a champion? The sorrow of Edward's death had crushed her to an emotional flatness she'd never experienced before. Simply staying alive took every ounce of strength and effort she could muster.

Mr. Lamkin adjusted the papers in front of him. "Well, then, let's begin." He cleared his throat. "As you know, Mrs. Vye, your husband's recent trip to London was the result of a serious financial downturn."

Loretta stiffened. "Yes. He mentioned as much to me before his departure. Frankly, his announcement left me quite bewildered and perplexed." She sighed. "But I trusted Edward."

Mr. Lamkin's eyes filled with sorrow. "His intention in his will was to leave you everything. At the time of drawing it up, he did not know, of course, what 'everything' would include. It was his intent to leave you with your current dwelling plus a handsome sum of money that would suffice you for the rest of your life and even allow you to bequeath a financial legacy to the person or persons of your choice."

Loretta tightened her grip on the cross as she thought of Molly and Sean. How wonderful it would be to leave them a financial legacy after her death.

Mr. Lamkin paused, his compassionate gaze intent upon her. "Mrs. Vye, it is with the deepest regret that I must inform you that your husband's last trip to London resulted in a declaration of bankruptcy. Before his departure from Liverpool, he sent me a telegram notifying me of his failed attempts to save his assets." He paused, as though measuring her reaction. "I am afraid to inform you that you are virtually destitute."

Loretta went limp, all breath sucked from her lungs. Mr. Lamkin's dictum rang in her ears. Destitute. Virtually destitute. She gripped the arms of her chair and fought against the blackness that dropped before her eyes.

"Are you all right, Mrs. Vye?"

She must not faint. She would not faint. She struggled to regain her composure. "Forgive me, Mr. Lamkin, but how could you ask if I am all right after what you just told me?"

Compunction colored Mr. Lamkin's face. "I meant no harm, Mrs. Vye. It is simply my duty as your husband's attorney to convey to you the truth of your situation."

She lowered her eyes. "I understand. And I'm sorry for my impertinence."

"No need to apologize. I would certainly feel the same way were I in your position."

But he wasn't. She was all alone in her position. Loretta's stomach sank to her feet. Although Edward's sudden death had blindsided her, the financial situation in which he'd left her now demolished every last shred of hope she'd clung to.

"But whatever shall I do?" Were Edward alive, she could vent her anger upon him. But, to her great dismay, his ears were beyond her protests. "What about my house? Do I get to keep my house?"

Mr. Lamkin cleared his throat. "I'm afraid not. Your husband had placed your house as collateral against his debts. In other words, your husband secured his debt with your house. Your husband's creditors, therefore, have demanded that the house and everything in it—except your personal belongings, of course—be used to pay off his debt."

"You can't be serious." The cold hands of panic gripped her by the throat.

Mr. Lamkin nodded. "I am so sorry, Mrs. Vye, but I could not be more serious."

"But why am I responsible for my husband's business debts, especially since I had no awareness of them?"

"Unfortunately, Mrs. Vye, when you and your husband married, you agreed to take on each other's debts. There is no stipulation in Edward's will to vindicate you from the satisfaction of his debts upon his death."

Heat rose to Loretta's face as regret flooded her. "Unfortunately, you are right, Mr. Lamkin. I did, indeed, sign such an agreement." She choked back a sob. "Never expecting that should Edward die with an outstanding debt, there would be not be sufficient provision to pay it off."

Hot bile burned her throat. Mother had been right again. A woman should never trust her financial future to a man. Nor any aspect of her future, for that matter.

Mr. Lamkin shook his head. "You have my deepest sympathy, Mrs. Vye."

Loretta rose and paced the office, fire burning in her belly. "I don't want your sympathy, Mr. Lamkin. What good will your sympathy do me? I need some advice. I have nowhere to turn." She tried to stop the trembling from taking over her body. But to no avail.

"I wish I could offer you some advice." His admission came out tentative, apologetic.

She faced him squarely. "But where shall I live? Have his creditors no mercy for a poor widow?"

Visibly, the lawyer swallowed.

She mustered her courage. "Dare I ask, Mr. Lamkin, the amount of the debt?"

He hesitated. "Ten thousand dollars."

Loretta's blood froze. "Impossible! I cannot repay it. Don't you understand I have nothing?" The few coins left in her purse would buy her only her next meal. Or, perhaps, her last.

"I must regretfully add that the house and all its contents are insufficient to fulfill his financial obligations."

How could Edward have accrued such massive debt? And without having told her about any of it? Fear wrestled with anger on the platform of her heart. The room around her spun. This could not be. Surely, this was only a bad dream.

"I am, therefore—" Her voice broke. She struggled

to compose herself. "I am, therefore, reduced to nothing."

"I'm sorry, Mrs. Vye. But that fact does not exonerate you from fulfilling Edward's debt."

"And if I can't?" She stopped abruptly in front of his desk and slapped a palm on it. "Is there no mercy for a widow? Surely my husband's creditors cannot expect payment when I have nothing with which to pay them." Her voice cracked.

"I will do what I can for you, Mrs. Vye. It all depends on the responses of the creditors."

All breath drained from Loretta's lungs. She collapsed into the chair and dropped her hands onto her lap. Numbness gripped her soul. "Very well, then, what do you suggest I do while we wait?"

Mr. Lamkin's gaze met hers. "I suggest you find a relative or friend who can help you in providing you with food and shelter. And, perhaps, in contributing to the repayment of your debt."

The thought of begging for money filled her with the utmost shame and disgust. She would never subject herself to such utter humiliation. Oh, if Edward were still alive, she'd give him a huge piece of her mind. "Has it truly come to this? Have I been reduced to abject poverty? And that, with the simple stroke of a pen?"

He ignored her questions. "I further suggest that you find yourself some employment whereby you can earn your keep and provide for yourself." He hesitated. "Thirdly, if the first two options do not materialize, I suggest you look for another husband."

Loretta bolted upright in the chair. Her breath caught. The insult! "Are you suggesting, Mr. Lamkin, that a woman cannot survive without a husband?"

Mr. Lamkin shifted. "I am not suggesting that at all, Mrs. Vye. But, truth be told, how many women do you know who can support themselves financially?"

His words caused her blood to boil. She rose, tapping into a courage deep within her, a courage implanted in her by her mother. A courage that Aunt Martha's hateful, condescending attitude had buried and nearly destroyed.

She fastened her gaze on the attorney. "Mr. Lamkin, you are looking at a woman who will prove to you—and to the entire world, if necessary—that I do not need the support of a man, nor will I accept it. Furthermore, I will pay off my late husband's debt and remain honorable to my good name." She lowered her voice. "Whatever is left of it."

His mouth slightly agape, the attorney blinked at her.

Lifting her chin, Loretta shoved her reticule under

her arm. "Good day, Mr. Lamkin." With that, she took her leave, closing the door a little more forcefully than was proper for a lady.

Thursday, April 3, 1873

How dare Mr. Lamkin insinuate that the solution to her problem was a husband? It was just like a man to do so. Why did men consider women second-class citizens? Yes, women were generally weaker physically, but women were far stronger than men morally, psychologically, and emotionally. Mr. Lamkin's comment only served to reveal his obtuseness. The very nerve of him!

Her stomach roiling, Loretta continued along the sidewalk to her home. A light wind whistled through the budding trees while gray clouds floated overhead. April in New Jersey was known for its showers, and one seemed quite imminent.

She quickened her pace, eager to reach home before a downpour. She had reached the midpoint of her walk when a soft whimper caught her attention. She stopped to look around. Perhaps an animal had been injured.

Not finding anything, Loretta resumed her walk when the whimper came again, this time more loudly. Her gaze carefully scanned the area and fell on a small child—a boy—sitting under a sycamore tree. His head was buried in his hands, and he was crying.

Loretta's heart filled with compassion. She approached the child and stooped down. He wore a tattered shirt, and the soles of his shoes were filled with holes. "What's wrong, little one?"

"My mama and I have nothing to eat. She sent me to look for food. She's at home doing laundry and mending for the neighbors to earn some money."

"Have you no father?"

"No, ma'am. He left us when I was three."

Loretta's chest constricted. "How old are you now?"

"I'm five, almost six."

"Do you live nearby?"

He pointed to a structure a few steps away. "I live in that gray house."

Loretta followed the trajectory of his finger to a house where the shutters hung askew, the paint was peeling, and the wooden frame displayed several cracks.

She returned her gaze to the child. "I'm so sorry your father left you." She reached into her purse and drew out the last few coins she possessed. "Here, child.

Take this home to your mother and buy yourselves some food."

The boy wiped the tears from his eyes. "Thank you, ma'am. Mama will be so grateful."

Loretta tousled his hair. "I'm sure she will." She paused, an ache forming in her soul. "I wish I could do more for you."

The boy rose to his feet. "You've done so much, ma'am. Thank you." He gave Loretta a big hug.

Tears welled up in her eyes. "Your father may have left you, dear child, but always remember that you have a Father in heaven who will never leave you." But why did she have trouble believing this for herself as well?

The boy smiled and ran off, shouting, "Mama! Mama! Wait till you hear what just happened?"

Loretta whispered a prayer for the boy and his mother and then resumed her walk home.

By the time she arrived, Molly had left for the day. A note lay on the kitchen counter. *"Mrs. Vye, I've completed my duties for the day. I will see you in the morning, Molly."*

As much as she loved Molly, Loretta was glad to be alone. The ordeal at Mr. Lamkin's office had left her quite shaken. She needed time alone to sort out her feelings and to plan her next step.

Chapter Seven

Friday, April 4, 1873

Paper and pencil in hand, Jeremiah sat at his table and tallied his sales for the week. Business had doubled since the first of the year. Praise the Lord! He'd soon need to hire someone to help him handle the onslaught of customers that filled his store every day, some from as far away as Cumberland and Salem Counties. Although he was pleased, some of the customers had started to complain at the long wait time in the purchase line. Not a good thing. He'd have to fix that, and fix it soon. He'd put up a *Help Wanted* sign in front of his store in the hope of finding a good, trustworthy man to lift some of the load.

Burrows jumped onto the table, right smack in the middle of Jeremiah's ledger. "Whoa, Burrows!" Jeremiah sighed. "You know better than to jump up here while I'm doing my arithmetic." He lifted the cat from the ledger page which she had wrinkled with her paw. "You must be trying to tell me you're hungry, right?"

Burrows purred, jumped down from the table, and scrambled toward the kitchen.

Jeremiah followed her and took a container of dried fish off the shelf. Before he could even finish putting the food in the cat's bowl, she was on top of it, gulping it down like a starving wild animal.

Jeremiah straightened and chuckled. "I guess you really were hungry." He scratched his head. "Next time, give me a warning, will you? I may have to record that page of my ledger all over again."

While Burrows finished her lunch, Jeremiah finished his figuring. At noon, he closed the shop for his lunch break and then headed to the post office to retrieve his mail.

On his way, he stopped to purchase the day's paper. News about the shipwreck of the *S.S. Atlantic* continued to trickle in as more and more information leaked about the exact cause of the tragedy. Seemed as though negligence had played a big part in the deaths of hundreds of people, making the calamity even more painful. It was bad enough when a tragedy could not have been avoided, but when it could have, it became all the more tragic.

Despite its status as one of the most advanced steamships afloat, the *SS Atlantic* had fallen prey to human error–something Jeremiah himself, as a former trawler captain, had had to contend with. According to one report, had it not been for the quick thinking and bravery of the fishermen living in the small community of Lower Prospect, where the ship had crashed into the rocks, many more lives would have been lost.

Jeremiah folded the newspaper and tucked it under his arm. The day was bright and breezy as he covered the two blocks to the post office. A brilliant sun graced a blue, cloudless sky. Houses along the way sported open windows and gardens filled with budding daffodils and stately tulips. Here and there, a housewife hung the family wash on a clothesline in the backyard while humming a lilting tune.

Jeremiah took in a long breath of the fresh air and climbed the five steps to the post office entrance. The old building was a gathering place for local news. Each day at noon, locals would gather to collect their mail and to catch up on the latest gossip.

"Good afternoon, Jeremiah." Henry, the postmaster greeted him with a smile. "Nice day today."

Jeremiah smiled. "Beautiful. One of the nicest we've had this spring."

Henry reached behind him and grabbed a small pile of mail. "All ready for you." He handed the bundle to Jeremiah. "You're as punctual as my old Swiss pocket watch."

Jeremiah laughed. "That's good to know. My papa taught me always to be on time."

The postmaster chuckled. "He taught you well. Wish more of today's young whippersnappers would learn that lesson."

Jeremiah nodded. "Seems like old values are fast disappearing."

"I hear you. I also hear your fishing supply store is fast becoming one of the main tourist attractions in town."

Jeremiah raised an eyebrow. "Is that so? Perhaps that's the reason business has been so good. I'm now a tourist attraction. Who would have thought?"

Henry joined in the laughter. "Seems like our little town is growing in fame and popularity. Doesn't surprise me."

"Nor me. Cape May is a beautiful place to live."

"Well, whatever the reason, a growing business is a

good thing."

"Yes. It's spurring me to hire some help soon. I'm having trouble serving the customers in a timely fashion. Frankly, it concerns me. I want to be a good steward of the business God has given me."

The postmaster's gazed locked on to Jeremiah's "Just the fact that you have that attitude shows you're a good steward."

Jeremiah changed the subject. "So have you heard anything more about the shipwreck?"

The postmaster shook his head. "Nothing more than that each day, more and more victims are being found. Sadly, one of them, at least, was from New Jersey."

"So I heard. Did you know any of them?"

"No, but I understand the New Jersey victim was a certain Edward Vye, a railroad tycoon from Cape May. He left behind a widow."

"A shame. Any children?"

"None that I know of."

A young man moved toward the counter to retrieve his mail.

Jeremiah gave a nod to the postmaster. "I'd best be going. You've got other people to tend to."

He gave Jeremiah a wave and proceeded to attend to the young man.

With a pile of mail in his hand, Jeremiah headed back to his store, all the while thinking about the widow who'd lost her husband in the shipwreck. Perhaps he could do something to ease her suffering. After all, he'd lost a spouse and knew what that was like.

And only those who'd been there truly understood.

Thursday, April 10, 1873

Loretta sat at her dressing table, her head spinning. She had so much to think about. At the top of her mental list was Molly. Loretta could no longer afford to employ the dear girl. Molly would have to find a new job, and Loretta wanted to help her. The least she could do was write a glowing letter of recommendation. Perhaps one of the ladies of her knitting circle needed a maid or knew of someone who did.

Then there was the matter of the hounding creditors. Mr. Sloan, leader of the pack, had visited her a couple of times to explain the process of repossession.

"I advise you to go through your personal belongings and remove them. Items like clothing and books. Those you may keep."

Her heart lurched. "What about my jewelry?"

He hesitated. "I'm sorry, but all jewelry is included in the repossession."

Loretta's breath caught. She grabbed the cross around her neck. "You can take everything except this cross." Her voice quivered. "It was a gift from my mother when I was but a child. She gave it to me shortly before she died." She could barely speak over the aching lump in her throat.

Mr. Sloan was visibly moved. "You may keep the cross since it was yours before you married Mr. Vye."

What else was hers before she'd married Edward? Very little but the clothing on her back and a few precious volumes. She'd come to this marriage with nothing. She was leaving it with nothing.

She sat at her dressing table and stared at her reflection in the mirror. In the past few weeks, she'd changed from a youthful-looking forty-year-old woman to a haggard middle-aged widow. Pronounced lines framed her eyes that had lost their light. Her sallow skin, once clear and rosy, now looked ashen.

Tears welled up in her eyes. Never in her wildest dreams had she thought her life would come to this. How had she gotten here? If anyone had warned her only a few months ago that she would be destitute and homeless, she would have laughed in his face.

Yet here she was, as low as she could go. And with no prospect of recovery. With no hope in sight.

What had come of all her dependence on others? Her trusting others to take care of her? Every one of those she'd trusted had failed her in some way. Her parents had failed her by dying. Uncle Malcolm had failed her by not protecting her from Aunt Martha's cruel hatred, a hatred spawned by her aunt's jealousy that she could not bear a child as her sister, Loretta's mother, had. And Edward had failed her by leaving her destitute.

In every case, man had failed her.

Most of all, she'd failed herself by waiting for others to take care of her. What had happened to the young Loretta who knew how to take charge of a situation? The little girl who took on life with exuberant expectancy of success? Who never let an opportunity pass her by? Who waited for no one before plunging into the unknown? The little girl who had big dreams of conquering the world?

Now, she could not even conquer herself. She shook her head as hot tears watered her cheeks.

A shiver of disgust coursed through her veins.

Her mother used to tell her, "Loretta, you are a

natural-born leader." And when she'd been with her friends, it had proven true. Why was it, then, that she now could hardly do anything but put one foot in front of the other? Even that had become a challenge since Edward's death. From morning till night, she'd simply gone through the motions of living. She'd become like one of those new-fangled, wind-up mechanical dolls without a heart. Moving, but lifeless.

A million thoughts raced across the canvas of her mind. Why had she repeatedly allowed herself to be manipulated by strong-willed people like Aunt Martha? Why had she allowed herself to be treated with disrespect, unkindness, and even neglect? What major flaw within her had caused her to fail to stand up for herself?

She swallowed hard. Which Loretta was she really? The weak, dependent one who cowered at the least show of power? Or the brave, independent one who would let nothing stand in her way? The one who would allow no one to dictate who she was? No one to define her?

Her stomach muscles squeezed against her spine. What was holding her back from deciding? Was it fear? Self-hatred? A sense of unworthiness? A combination of all three?

She choked back the tears. Papa's last words to her

before the accident surfaced from the depths of her soul. *If you remember only one thing I say to you, my dear Loretta, remember this: no one can decide who you are but you yourself.*

The memory of her father's words ignited something deep within her. Something the sufferings caused by the oppressive people in her life had buried under a mound of lies about who she was. Lies she'd believed and allowed to control her life. Lies that had imprisoned her unawares. That was the way of lies. They were hidden, subtle, and unrelenting. They worked their harm unbeknownst to their victim.

It was her responsibility to determine who she was. The Lord had already given her worth by the very fact of creating her and dying for her. Yet, by disrespecting herself, she had insulted the Lord. In a sense, she'd slapped Him across the face by refusing to acknowledge that she was who He said she was. In effect, she'd called Him a liar.

She shuddered at the horrid realization. It called for repentance.

With tears streaming down her face, she bowed her heart before the God of the universe, thanking Him for having created her. Thanking Him for having forgiven her. Thanking Him for having kept her during the worst storms of her life.

But now, the decision lay before her. She searched her reflection in the mirror. What would it be? No one could make that decision for her without her permission. And, yet, that's precisely what she'd done after her parents' death—allowed others to define her. To dictate who she was and who she could be. And she'd died on the inside as a result.

Loretta drew in a long breath. A deep knowing rose big within her. She alone was at fault for her dependent attitude. It had nothing to do with her financial situation. Or her marital situation. Why hadn't she probed Edward about their finances? After all, she was his wife. She'd had the right to know, but instead, she'd viewed herself as helpless, and that's what she'd become.

A Scripture verse surfaced from the depths of her heart. *As a man thinks, so is he*. Mama had her memorize that verse shortly after Loretta had been born again. Why hadn't she put it into practice?

It was about time she turned the tables and started thinking of herself as God thought of her. Of looking at herself as the overcomer in Christ she truly was.

She swallowed a lump in her throat and wiped the tears from her eyes as courage flooded her soul. The time of reckoning had come. The time for making a decision. The point of no return.

Ebony's words came back to her. *God is faithful.. He's the only one who can truly help you. He's the only one who will never fail you.*

Maybe Ebony was right. Man had certainly failed her. But could she really trust God not to fail her? Hadn't He been the one to allow all the tragedies in her life? Could He not have prevented them from happening? If so, why hadn't He?"

How had she gotten to this place? She'd gotten here by the grace and mercy of God. He'd allowed her to reach the end of her rope so that He could pull her out of the abyss.

From now on, with God's guidance, she alone would decide what was best for Loretta Vye. No longer would she allow any man to make her decisions for her. No longer would she cower before the pressure and demands of others.

She pressed her lips together. Leaving town was her only option. She'd increase her chances of finding work if she went to an area with more opportunity. But to leave behind everything she knew? Her friends? Her church? And hadn't Clarissa advised her to give herself another chance?

Maybe she'd follow Clarissa's advice and give herself another chance. She would start looking for work here in Cape May and pray God would provide.

* * *

Friday, April 11, 1873

Loretta's heart wrenched as Molly arrived for her last day of work. The maid's wages for the month had been paid before Edward's departure.

"Good morning, Molly."

"Top o' the mornin' to ya, Mrs. Vye." Tears glistened in the young maid's eyes as she gave Loretta a tentative smile. "How are you this mornin', ma'am?"

An ache lodged in Loretta's heart. "Miserable, Molly. Just plain miserable." She took Molly into her arms. "My dear girl, my heart breaks at having to let you go." She held her close for a moment and then released her. "I could not have asked for a better maid than you. May the good Lord bless you for your faithfulness over these many years."

"I'll be forever grateful to you, Mrs. Vye. Workin' for you has made me a better person."

Loretta was thankful that Molly had found employment with Miriam Goldstein, one of Loretta's friends from her knitting circle. "You'll be in good hands with Mrs. Goldstein."

"I'm sure I will, ma'am. I'll be startin' with her on Monday."

Loretta patted Molly's hand. "She's blessed to have you." Loretta had prepared a special gift for Molly's last day of work. "I baked you your favorite apple cake."

Oh, Mrs. Vye! How kind of you!"

"Take it home and enjoy it with Sean."

"He will love it." Molly wiped a tear from her eye. "I won't be leavin' forever, Mrs. Vye. We'll still be able to visit, right?"

"Of course! My home is always open to you." A sob caught in her throat. "I stand corrected. My heart is always open to you, dear Molly, no matter where I live."

"Sean and I been prayin' for you, ma'am. I know the Lord has good things in store for you."

As much as Loretta wanted to believe Molly's words, she found it difficult to do so. "I'm hoping He does." She paused and looked squarely at Molly. "You take good care of yourself, do you hear?"

Molly nodded. "I will, ma'am. And you do the same."

As Molly left with the cake in hand, Loretta pushed down the sob that had lodged in her throat.

Chapter Eight

Thursday, April 17, 1873

Loretta sat in the back pew of her little country church. The ladies would soon convene in the Sunday school room. She'd arrived early to spend a few moments in prayer in the sanctuary before joining them.

As Loretta gazed at the Cross hanging above the altar in front of her, Mama's words echoed within her soul. *The Lord is a very present help in time of trouble, Loretta. He will always take care of you.*

Well, here she was, bankrupt and with no means of supporting herself. Would God come through for her?

"Loretta." Clarissa slipped into the pew and sat

down beside her. “I noticed you sitting here as I walked in the front door.” She placed a hand on Loretta's arm. “How are you doing?”

Loretta turned toward Clarissa, a lump in her throat. “I'm worried sick about my future. I own nothing and have no means of supporting myself.” She sighed. “Absolutely none.”

Clarissa shook her head. “I'm so sorry. You must feel very frightened.” She took Loretta’s hand.

“Worse than that. I feel hopeless.” Loretta choked back a sob. “I’ve asked around town if anyone is hiring. I’ve looked in the newspaper advertisements. I’ve spent the last several days inquiring about different types of work. I’ve offered my services as a nanny, a cook, a seamstress, and a cleaning woman, to no avail. All doors have closed.” A nervous laugh escaped her lips. “I suppose I could become a washerwoman.” She imagined herself giving away all her lovely dresses and donning the drab garb of that lowly trade.

“Well, there's certainly nothing wrong with being a washerwoman. It's an honorable job. But I don't think the earnings would be enough to support you.” Clarissa gave her a kindly smile. “Surely the Lord will make a way for you.”

Loretta tensed. “Well, He'd better do it in short

order, or I will soon be eating my last meal." A tear trickled down her cheek.

Clarissa placed an arm around Loretta's shoulder. "Come now. You have us to help you. We're your friends and sisters in Christ, Loretta. You know that we will never allow you to starve." She gave Loretta's shoulder a squeeze and smiled.

Heat rose to Loretta's face. While she greatly appreciated her friend's offer, how humiliating that there was a need for it. "You've already helped so much, what with all the meals you and the knitting circle ladies have brought me. Plus, you've provided me with shelter until I get back on my feet and find a place to live."

Loretta's heart warmed. Yes, she could count on her knitting circle to help her through this ordeal. But she needed to find a way to support herself. The women had their own families to take care of and couldn't worry about her.

Clarissa rose. "It's time for knitting circle to begin. Ebony and Miriam are already here. We're still waiting for Ornella and Cholena. Maybe they will have some ideas for you."

Loretta picked up her knitting supplies from the pew. "I hope so. I've exhausted every possibility I've tried." Reluctantly, she followed Clarissa to the Sunday school room.

When Loretta entered, Ebony Phillips and Miriam Goldstein were already seated and knitting up a storm.

"Hello, Loretta." Ebony gave her a brilliant smile. "So glad to see you."

"Thank you. It's nice to see you, too, Ebony."

"Shalom, Loretta. We've missed you." Miriam muttered through a stitch marker between her lips.

"Shalom to you, too, Miriam."

Loretta found her usual place at the round table, between Ebony and Miriam. "That's a lovely scarf you're knitting, Miriam."

The multi-colored yarn moved like a melody through Miriam's expert fingers. "Thank you." She looked up at Loretta. "So how are you doing?"

Loretta placed her bag on the table and then sat down. "As well as can be expected, I guess."

"I hear you." Miriam did not miss a stitch as her needles rapidly clicked away. "When my Jacob died, I thought the world had come to an end."

Before Loretta could ask the question on her mind, Miriam spoke again. "Thanks to Adonai, Jacob left me enough money to live on for the rest of my life. Otherwise, I don't know what I would have done."

"I wish I could say the same for myself."

Miriam stopped in the middle of a stitch and turned her gaze toward Loretta. "It's that serious, is it? What do you plan to do?"

Loretta swallowed hard. "I've been praying and asking God for direction. I've been exploring job opportunities here in Cape May, but every door has closed thus far."

Ebony jumped in. "Well, you've turned to the right place in turning to the Lord."

Loretta stiffened. If she were honest, she questioned whether God knew what she was going through. And if He knew, did He even care?

"The Lord is all you need."

"I suppose so."

Ebony's eyebrows shot straight up. "You *suppose* so?"

While Ebony meant well, she was quick to maximize the spiritual side of life and minimize the practical. Yet Loretta couldn't deny that Ebony's unwavering faith had gotten her through many a seemingly impossible trial. Secretly, Loretta wished she had her friend's staunch faith.

Ebony waved a knitting needle in the air. "Don't you remember the story about how Jesus fed five thousand people, not including women and children, with five loaves of bread and two fish? And there were twelve baskets of leftovers!"

Loretta nodded. She'd often heard the story as a child, sitting at her mother's knee. "But that happened when Jesus was on earth. He's no longer here."

Ebony flashed another brilliant smile. "His Holy Spirit is here. Besides, the Bible says that Jesus is the same yesterday, today, and forever." She resumed her knitting. "So that means he can multiply a loaf of bread for you today just as well as He did when He was on earth." Her laughter rippled throughout the room.

Loretta smiled in spite of herself and tucked that truth into the back of her mind. She might need it very soon.

"Well, good morning, ladies!" Cholena Cohanzick strolled into the room, smiling. "How is everyone today?"

"We're doing well, praise God." Ebony was the first to respond.

Clarissa's gaze traveled around the table. "Except for Loretta here."

Furrowing her brows, Cholena lowered herself into the chair opposite Loretta. "What's the matter, Loretta? Can we help in some way?"

Loretta sighed. "Well, so far no success in finding a job."

Cholena looked at her. "I'm so sorry to hear that.

We've been praying for you ever since Clarissa told us what happened."

"Not as sorry as I am." Loretta choked back the now-familiar tears. "The worst of it is that I've lost my house." A pain shot through her stomach. How she loved the house she and Edward had purchased when they'd first married nineteen years earlier. Losing it was like wrenching her soul from her body.

"There must be something you can do." Cholena drew her eyebrows together.

Ornella Lombardo, the last to arrive, walked through the door. "Hello, everyone."

Ornella placed her knitting bag at the last remaining place at the round table, at a diagonal from Loretta. "So, what's happening?" She turned toward Loretta. "Have you found a job yet, Loretta?"

"No. I've spent the last few days talking to numerous people, but no one was interested in hiring me."

Ornella gasped. "*Mamma mia*!" She always resorted to her native Italian language when upset. Ornella lowered her ample body into the chair. "Well, my dear Loretta, you've heard the old saying that two heads are better than one." She chuckled. "We have six heads here." She leaned toward Loretta. "Imagine what six heads can do."

As kind as Ornella's attempt to encourage her might be, it was doubtful that six heads could any more solve her problem than one.

Clarissa intervened. "It's time to begin, ladies." She had them bow their heads and prayed for wisdom for Loretta's situation and asked the Lord to provide direction for her. Everyone added their amens.

No sooner had Clarissa finished praying than Cholena turned toward Loretta. "I know what you can do."

Ebony cheered. "Well, that was the quickest answer to pray I've ever seen."

Hope sparking in her chest, Loretta gave her an attentive ear. "What?"

"Why not open a knitting shop?"

Loretta quirked up an eyebrow. "A knitting shop?"

Cholena nodded emphatically. "Yes! A knitting shop. You could sell yarn and other knitting supplies."

Miriam clapped her hands. "That's a brilliant idea! You're a fantastic knitter. You could even give knitting lessons."

Ornella giggled. "Who knows? In the future you could even expand your shop to include crochet, embroidery, and other needle arts."

"But I have no money to open a knitting shop."

Ever the practical one of the group, Clarissa gave

Loretta a reassuring smile. “Perhaps you should first find employment to get yourself back on your feet again and then think about opening a knitting shop.”

“That seems my only logical recourse at the moment. I need a job to provide a roof over my head and food in my pantry. Meanwhile, I could put aside some money to open a knitting shop later.”

“Precisely.” Clarissa nodded emphatically. “Have you found a place to live?”

Loretta cringed. She'd been so shocked over Edward's death and her subsequent discovery of bankruptcy that she hadn't yet looked for a place to live. But she'd better do so right away because Edward's creditors wanted her out of the house by the middle of the month.

“Not yet.” She tried to hide the quiver in her voice. She didn't even know where to start looking.

“Well, you could stay with me until you do,” Clarissa said.

“And with me, too.” One by one, each of the ladies offered their homes to Loretta. Her heart warmed.

“Thank you. You are all so dear to me.” Loretta paused. “After our meeting today, I plan to broaden my search. I'll even consider moving from Cape May.”

“Do you have a specific location in mind?” Cholena drew a new skein of blue yarn from her bag.

"Well, if I can't find work in Cape may, I do have a cousin in Atlanta, Georgia."

"Oh, I hope you can stay in this area, Loretta. You have your church family here."

Her church family. Yes. The wonderful people of her church had meant the world to her over the past several years. Despite their occasional annoying flaws, they'd always been there for her and Edward. It would take a lot for her to leave them.

"I, too, hope I can stay. That's my first choice. To stay in Cape May. I love this town. I love living near the ocean. I love the people." Loretta smiled. "And I love all of you."

Cholena suddenly stopped knitting. "This may sound farfetched, but on my way over here, I noticed a *Help Wanted* sign in front of Collins's Fishing Supply Store on Main Street. Perhaps you could apply there."

"A fishing supply store?" Miriam looked up in surprise. "Now, that's a novel idea." She turned toward Loretta. "Do you know anything about fishing?"

"Not a thing, except that I don't like it. But, when I was a little girl, my father once took me fishing in the bay, and I caught four flounder." Loretta chuckled at the memory.

Ebony slapped the table. "Now that's what I call

experience. After all, how many women can say they've caught four flounder?"

Loretta knit her brows. "I doubt it could be called fishing prowess, though."

Cholena lifted her chin. "Do you like to eat fish?"

"I love to eat certain fish."

Ornella jumped in. "Then that's all the qualification you need."

Loretta joined in the general laughter at Ornella's food-focused comment. Then she grew serious. Maybe this job opportunity was something she should consider. She had nothing to lose and, perhaps, something to gain.

She turned toward Cholena. "Did the sign say what kind of position the owner is looking to fill?"

Cholena shook her head. "No. The sign said only *Help Wanted*."

Loretta thought a moment. "That could mean anything." She sighed. "Well, I suppose it can't hurt to find out. Maybe the owner is looking for someone to clean the store or to stock the shelves."

Clarissa smiled. "Yes. Most certainly it's worth a try. Who knows but that God is making a way for you to provide for yourself and to move into the next phase of life He has planned for you."

Loretta could always count on Clarissa to offer a

word of encouragement. “I'll stop by the store today on my way home.”

A spark of hope flickered in Loretta's heart. But she would not fan it until she had a job in hand.

Thursday, April 17, 1873

After the knitting circle meeting, Loretta headed straight for Collin's Fishing Supply Store on Main Street. She had no time to lose. Eviction day was imminent.

Her heart raced as she approached the two-story, clapboard building. She stood in front of it for a moment. It was a simple structure, with a small front yard enclosed by a split-rail fence. A gate led from the sidewalk into the yard and up to the landing in front of the door. Two large windows, one on either side of the door, looked out upon the main street of town.

Loretta took a deep breath and smoothed the front of her long skirt. Her muscles tensed. What if she made a fool of herself? Fishing was a man's occupation. She'd likely be laughed out of the building in short order.

Mustering all the courage within her, she climbed

the three steps to the landing and placed a tentative hand on the doorknob. *Lord, help me. Give me favor if this is Your will for me.*

Taking a deep breath, she opened the door and entered. A bell tinkled, startling her.

She looked around. Except for a pretty calico cat that sat atop the windowsill, the place was empty. "Hello. Is anyone here?" She tried to still the tremor in her voice.

A rustling sound from a back room caught her attention. A man emerged and stood before her.

Loretta's breath caught. The man was extraordinarily handsome, tall and broad-shouldered, with dark, deep-set eyes, a strong Roman nose, and a neatly cropped beard. His salt-and-pepper hair was cut close to the sides of his head except for a thick thatch on top of his head. She guessed him to be in his mid-forties. With her reaction came a pang of guilt. What kind of woman was she? Her husband was still fresh in his grave at the bottom of the sea.

"Good day, ma'am." He greeted her with a broad smile that warmed her heart. "I'm Jeremiah Collins. How may I help you?"

Loretta swallowed hard, more from the first impression he'd made on her than from her nervousness regarding the job. "I saw your notice outside that you are hiring. I'm here to apply for the position."

He raised both eyebrows. "But you're a woman."

The hair rose at the nape of Loretta's neck. "I'm glad you noticed." She hadn't meant to be sarcastic, but ever since her conversation with Molly, the cultural inequality between men and women was a topic that roused her ire.

A smile edged the man's lips. "And a spunky one at that, I see." His gaze studied her. "What does a woman know about fishing?"

"I don't know what other women know, but I know nothing about fishing."

"Well, you're an honest woman, if nothing else."

Loretta bristled. "I can learn anything I need to learn."

He hesitated. "Look, ma'am, I appreciate your coming in, but there's no way I'm going to hire a woman to handle the gruff men that come into my shop, and especially not a woman who knows nothing about fishing. I'm afraid I cannot offer you the job."

Loretta's heart sank.

He bid her good day and started toward the back of the store.

"Please. Please wait a moment."

He turned. "I'm sorry, ma'am, but I don't have a moment to wait. Good day."

Loretta refused to leave. "Can you not at least have the decency to hear me out?"

Jeremiah raised an eyebrow. "Well, be quick about it. I have no time to waste."

She lifted her chin. "And neither do I. I am in dire straits and urgently need a solution."

He considered her for a moment. "Let's sit down." He pointed to the table with two chairs at the side of the shop.

Loretta sat down. "I desperately need a job. I recently lost my husband who left me in a state of financial bankruptcy." She lowered her gaze. "In a few days, I will be evicted from my home."

A glimmer of compassion reflected in his eyes. "I'm very sorry to hear that."

"I'm in desperate need of an income, and when I heard you were hiring, I thought I would apply." She didn't dare tell him she was down to her last dollar. Once that was gone, she would be on a path to starvation.

"Look, Mrs.—"

"Vye. Loretta Vye."

He stopped short. "Did you say 'Vye'? Your name is Vye?"

"Yes. Why do you ask?"

"I've heard that name somewhere before." He thought a moment. "Yes. Now I remember. Did you lose your husband in the recent shipwreck of the *SS Atlantic*?"

Her eyes moistened. "Yes. How did you know?"

"A friend of mine mentioned that a woman from the area lost a loved one as a result of that catastrophe."

She stared at the scarred top of the table. "I am that woman."

His face softened. "Look, Mrs. Vye, I'm very sorry for your situation, but perhaps you should find work more suited to a woman. Like cleaning house, or cooking, or taking care of children."

She stiffened. "Is that the only kind of work you think women can do?" She lowered her eyes. "Besides, I've already looked into that type of work, but there are no openings in Cape May."

He blew out a long breath but did not reply.

"Mr. Collins, I have exhausted all possibilities in our area. Few people are hiring due to the downward-turning economy."

"Yes, I am aware of that." He gave her a long, hard look. "I empathize with your plight, Mrs. Vye—truly I do—but I'm afraid I still cannot offer you the job. I need someone who knows the fishing industry and who can help my customers. Besides, I don't know how my male customers would take to a woman in a man's field." He averted his gaze. "I'm afraid you just won't do."

Loretta's heart crashed to her feet. No use persisting. The man had made up his mind. "Very well, then." She rose. "I pray you find someone suited to your needs."

Jeremiah stood. "Thank you." He hesitated. "I wish you the best, Mrs. Vye."

She nodded and then left, her heart shattered with despair. If he truly wished her the best, he would have hired her.

Thursday, April 17, 1873

No sooner had Mrs. Vye left than Tom Brogan walked into Jeremiah's store. He pushed his cap farther back on his head. "Howdy, Jeremiah."

"Hello, Tom."

Tom pointed toward the door. "Who was that good-lookin' woman I just passed on my way in here?"

"Oh. No one special." A pang of guilt piercedJeremiah's belly. Mrs. Vye had, indeed, struck him in what he couldn't deny was a special way. A profound way.

"Well, she was sure somethin' to look at, I'll say." Tom distanced himself from Burrows who had jumped onto the counter. "Was she shoppin' for somethin' for her husband?"

"No." Jeremiah hesitated. "She was applying for a job."

Tom laughed uproariously. "A woman workin' in a fishin' supply store?"

Jeremiah joined in the laughter, the pang of guilt digging more deeply into his conscience. "That's precisely what I thought."

"So why is she needin' a job?"

"She's a widow, and her husband left her with nothing."

Tom slammed his fist on the counter. "The scoundrel! Looks like that pretty woman be needin' a new husband, not a new job."

To his surprise, an arrow of jealousy pierced Jeremiah's soul. Why should he be jealous that Tom would be interested in a woman Jeremiah didn't even know?

Tom looked at Jeremiah with a twinkle in his eye. "If you don't go after her, I will."

Tom's challenge pricked Jeremiah's conscience even more. Had he been wrong to refuse Mrs. Vye an opportunity to survive? Should he have offered her the job? Would she now be homeless because of his unkindness and lack of compassion?

'“A man's a fool who lets a perty thing like that slip by.” The cat hissed as Tom shooed her off the counter.

Jeremiah flinched. A fool. The moniker fit him perfectly. He'd been a fool in letting Mrs. Vye go. He should have followed his better instincts and hired her. But how could he find her now? He'd gotten only her name. Would that be enough to locate her? What if she were forced to leave town because of her circumstances?

Jeremiah rubbed his head. “I have no idea where she lives.”

“Well, she must live here in Cape May since she applied for a job here.”

Jeremiah nodded. “Makes sense.”

Tom smiled. “I'll tell you what. Good friend that I am, I'll help you out. But I'm warnin' you, Jeremiah, once we find her, if you don't go after her, I will.”

Tom’s comment rubbed Jeremiah the wrong way. To his surprise, it aroused a sense of competitiveness within him. Like Tom, Jeremiah had not failed to notice Mrs. Vye’s femininity. The beauty of her face. The shapeliness of her body. Truth be told, she’d aroused his interest in a surprisingly unexpected way.

"Let's make a deal, Tom. I'll pursue her first. If she doesn't like me, I'll send her over to you." Despite a chuckle, he secretly hoped he'd find the lady and that she would give him the time of day. Especially after he'd shown little compassion in turning her down in her time of direst need.

Tom extended a hand. "Sounds like a fair deal to me." He grew serious. "Now, I'm holdin' you to it, you hear? You have one month to win her heart. If you don't, it will be my turn."

Jeremiah looked Tom straight in the eye. "You really mean this, don't you?"

"Of course, I do. There's something special about that lady. I could sense it in my bones when I walked by her. And I ain't stupid enough to miss an opportunity."

So Tom wasn't joking. Well, if Tom didn't consider it a joke, then neither would he.

Chapter Nine

Thursday, April 17, 1873

After Tom departed, Jeremiah could not get Mrs. Vye off his mind. To say the least, she was lovely to a level of perfection he'd rarely seen in a woman. Not only that, she aroused his protective instinct in a way that demanded action. But action without premeditation could lead to destruction. While her plight had touched him, he couldn't risk his business on a fleeting moment of emotion. Especially emotion for a woman. He knew himself well enough to know that his impulsiveness could get him into a lot of trouble.

Truth be told, Loretta Vye had intrigued him and caught his fancy from the instant he'd laid eyes on her.

Both her beauty and her spunk had ignited emotions he hadn't experienced ever since his youth, not since he'd first met Anna Mae.

But he had to be practical, didn't he? His business was his livelihood, and he couldn't risk doing something that would diminish his chances for success. And a woman would do just that. The kind of men who frequented his store would laugh and scoff at him for hiring a woman. They would accuse him of having lost his mind. No. Hiring Loretta Vye would do more harm than good for his business.

At the same time, he'd liked her feistiness and her willingness to learn. Far too many men lacked both traits.

As he arranged a display of fishing rods, a strange thought struck Jeremiah. Maybe a female clerk would attract business instead of repelling it. The novelty of having a woman in the store could create a stir and draw customers. Hadn't Tom suggested that very thing? Was Jeremiah willing to take the risk? Mrs. Vye did say she was willing to learn. He could teach her the fundamentals of fishing supplies, enough to answer basic questions, take customer orders, and fill them. Most of the time, customers chose what they wanted from the shelf anyway. All Mrs. Vye would have to do would be to write up the order, receive payment for it, and package the items.

Compassion wrestled with common sense in Jeremiah's soul. Had he truly heard from God, or were his emotions playing tricks on him? Hiring Mrs. Vye would give him continual proximity to her. He'd have a major advantage over Tom in their common desire to pursue the lovely widow.

But was he ready to pursue a relationship with a woman? Would doing so betray his love for Anna Mae? Would doing so hurt his business?

He shook his head. No. It wouldn't work. Better get rid of the idea now, before it took root. Collins's Fishing Supply Store was a man's world.

And Jeremiah determined to keep it that way.

Thursday, April 17, 1873

Her heart heavy, Loretta walked the two remaining blocks to her house. The day was overcast, portending a spring storm. In the distance, the rumble of thunder shook the sky.

She quickened her steps, her own world shaken by

Mr. Collins's refusal to hire her. It had cut her to the quick. This job was her last hope. Her last resort. What would she do now?

She reached her house, the house she'd grown to love. The only house she'd lived in after her marriage to Edward. It held so many happy memories. In a few days, it would be repossessed by Edward's creditors. In a few days, she would have to leave. But where would she go?

Never before had she experienced such loneliness.

She stood before the lovely Victorian structure, with its wide front porch and blue, shuttered windows. Already the forsythia had begun to bloom at the sides of the house, while the azaleas were preparing to make their bright and brilliant entrance on the stage of her front garden.

She climbed the steps and sat down in the old rocking chair. A wave of grief washed over her heart, crashing against her soul in an outburst of hot tears. *Oh, Edward! Edward! Edward! How can I go on without you?*

Loretta reached deep down inside and grabbed hold of the last thread of hope within her. A whisper escaped her lips. "Lord, help me. I'm at the end of my rope. I don't know where to turn."

A swallow landed on the porch railing in front of her and stared at her.

A swallow does not escape My notice. Neither do you.

A lump formed in Loretta's throat. God had not forgotten her. Yet she'd forgotten Him. She'd allowed herself to look to man to solve her problems instead of looking to God, the only One who could solve her problem. *Forgive me, Lord!*

She rose and went inside to pack. She did not have much time before the creditors would seize her house and all her belongings. It was already Thursday, and they would be arriving on Monday to repossess everything. She needed to have a place to stay by then. She would have to leave all the furnishings behind as well as the lovely jewelry Edward had purchased for her over the years. All she could keep would be her clothes. And her mother's cross.

She stifled a sob. How had her life come to this? Had she not suffered enough in losing her parents and living with a cruel aunt? Why was God punishing her like this? What had she done to deserve His wrath?

She wiped away the tears that trickled down her cheeks. It was hard not to be angry with God. And with Edward. Why had he left her in such a horrible situation? The fact that Edward was dead made her frustration even worse. She had no place to which to direct her anger. It just festered within her, eating away at her insides.

A knock on the door interrupted her thoughts. Putting aside the items she was packing, she went to answer.

A man stood before her, a hat in his hand. "Mrs. Vye?"

"Yes. I'm Mrs. Vye."

"I'm Wilbur Sloan from the collection agency."

Loretta's muscles stiffened. "I wasn't expecting you until Monday."

"You are correct. I've simply come to notify you that the repossession crew will be here promptly at eight o'clock Monday morning to repossess your belongings."

Loretta gave a strident laugh. "*My* belongings? Surely you jest. They are now *your* belongings."

The man's face grew taut. "Legally not until Monday, ma'am."

"Very well. I will expect you early Monday morning." She started to close the door.

The man lifted an index finger. "I must add, Mrs. Vye, that you will be requested to leave shortly after the men arrive. Please be sure to remove your clothing which, of course, you may keep."

"Oh, that is very kind of you." Her voice dripped

with sarcasm. She looked him up and down. "I suppose my wardrobe will not do *you* any good. Perhaps your wife would like to have it?" The instant she spoke the words, she regretted them. The man standing before her was not to blame for her bankruptcy. Edward was.

Mr. Sloan's expression pinched. "Mrs. Vye, I understand your bitterness at what has happened, and I am very sorry for your situation. But I am simply doing my job in alerting you. As of Monday morning, you will officially be without a home, so I suggest you find some lodging immediately."

Loretta's blood turned to ice. The moment of truth had come, and there was no turning back. "Please accept my apology for my rudeness. As you say, you are simply doing your job. It's just that—." Why try to explain? The man standing before her must have witnessed so many bankruptcies that he'd grown immune to them.

"Apology accepted." He lowered his eyes and then raised them again. "Might I add, Mrs. Vye, that no matter how many of these visits I've made over the years, it never gets any easier."

A wave of remorse flooded Loretta's soul.

"I'm just the messenger, if you will, ma'am."

She nodded. "Yes. You're just the messenger." She

paused. "I'm in the process of packing my clothing and a few personal items now. Everything will be ready by the time your crew arrives on Monday morning."

"Thank you. Very well, then. I shall take my leave until Monday. I wish you a pleasant day." He turned and left.

Loretta closed the door and leaned against it. Her world had come to an end. At least, her world as she'd known it. It was time to make a change. She would not allow herself to wallow in despair or self-pity. She would find a way. Didn't Mama always say that if there's a will, there's a way? Well, she certainly had the will. Now she'd have to find the way.

And find it she would.

* * *

Saturday, April 19, 1873

Jeremiah couldn't sleep. He tossed and turned on his narrow cot, his conscience piercing him with sharp arrows. He'd been a fool to turn Mrs. Vye away. He'd allowed the fear of man to stand in the way of compassion and common sense. The poor widow needed a chance. And he'd refused to give her one. What kind of man was he?

But now it was too late. She'd probably left town or found some other employment. He'd likely never see her again.

He drew in a deep breath, bunched up his pillow, and buried his head in it. If only she'd come back, he'd be willing to swallow his pride and recant his refusal. But why would she even consider coming back, after the way he'd treated her?

His toes brushed against Burrows, sleeping at the foot of the bed. The cat stirred and meowed and then went back to sleep. He was thankful she didn't wake up and want something to eat.

Jeremiah turned onto his back, trying to get comfortable. But he couldn't. No matter what, he had to find Mrs. Vye. Not just to offer her the job, but also to quell the longing for her in his heart that increased day by day.

He needed a plan. He searched his brain for a way to locate her. He'd start by going to the post office. Although the postmaster was not permitted to give out personal information, he might be able to point Jeremiah in the right direction.

The clock on the bookshelf struck three a.m. Another two hours before he'd get up. Jeremiah groaned. If he didn't get some sleep, he'd be exhausted the next day.

Burrows stirred, stretched, and stood up in the bed. She meowed and jumped onto the floor, waiting at the side of the bed for Jeremiah.

He looked down at her. "Don't tell me you're hungry again!"

Burrows sauntered over to the shelf and looked up at Jeremiah.

He chuckled. "I guess you are." He took a chunk of fish scraps down from the shelf and placed them in Burrows's bowl. "There you go." He straightened. "Well, since I'm up, I might as well stay up. No use tossing and turning in bed all night."

After dressing and making himself a cup of strong coffee, Jeremiah sat down at the table to read his Bible. He opened to the Book of Proverbs, and his eyes fell on Proverbs 21:13: *Whoso stoppeth his ears at the cry of the poor, he also shall cry himself, but shall not be heard.*

Guilt engulfed his soul. That's exactly what he'd done to Mrs. Vye. He'd stopped his ears at her cry. She'd told him she'd lost everything through her husband's bankruptcy. She was, indeed, poor. Jeremiah buried his head in his hands. Hot tears welled up in his eyes. "O God, have mercy on me. I have sinned against

You and Your Word in denying Mrs. Vye a job. Please forgive me."

As Jeremiah repented, peace settled over him. The Lord's promise in 1 John 1:9 rose from the depths of his spirit: *If we confess our sins, he is faithful and just to forgive us our sins, and to cleanse us from all unrighteousness.*

"Thank You, Lord, for forgiving me and for cleansing me. And now I ask, in the Name of Jesus, that, if it be Your will, please help me find Mrs. Vye." He closed his eyes. "Amen."

By the time he'd finished praying, dawn had stretched her long arms over the eastern sky, embracing it with her mantle of pink, blue, and gold. Jeremiah rose to fix himself a breakfast of eggs, bacon, and bread. After eating, he donned his cap and headed to the center of town to purchase the morning newspaper.

When he read an entry on the business page, his heart nearly stopped. *Position Wanted. Contact L. Vye at Post Office Box 39, Cape May, New Jersey.*

He couldn't believe his eyes. Mrs. Vye must truly be desperate to have placed the advertisement. It meant that she had not yet found a job and that she was still in the area.

His heart leapt with joy. The Lord had answered his prayer and had done so quickly.

Tucking the paper under his arm, he breathed a word of thanksgiving to God. As soon as he got home, he'd write a letter to Mrs. Vye, offering her the job. And he'd include an offer to live in the small, second-floor apartment as part of her pay.

Whether she'd accept or not remained to be seen. But, given her situation, she might not have any choice.

When Jeremiah arrived home, he found Burrows nestled in her favorite spot on the windowsill. He petted her and then went to his desk in the back of the store to get paper and his quill pen.

He sat down at his desk and wrote a short note informing Mrs. Vye that he was replying in response to her advertisement in the morning newspaper and that he was offering her the job after all. He signed his name, sealed and stamped the letter, and took it to the post office. He asked Henry the postmaster to put it in Mrs. Vye's mailbox. That done, his heart settled a bit.

Yet why did he fear that Mrs. Vye would reject his offer?

Chapter Ten

Chapter Ten

Monday, April 21, 1873

At eight o'clock sharp Monday morning, the creditors' wagon arrived. Loretta stood at the window as the large, lumbering vehicle pulled up in front of her house. Or, she should say, the creditors' house. Three weeks had passed since Edward's death.

Every muscle in her body tensed as the wagon came to an abrupt stop.

She moved away from the window, unwilling to be seen by the men. At their head was Wilbur Sloan, his face set like a flint toward the task at hand.

She opened the door before he had a chance to knock. "Good morning, Mr. Sloan."

"Good morning to you, too, Mrs. Vye. I trust you're doing well, considering the circumstances."

She did not reply. How well would Mr. Sloan be doing if his house were about to be repossessed?

"I suggest you leave before the work begins." He paused. "It will be less troubling for you, I believe."

"My bag is packed." She sighed. "Only one." She'd collected the clothing she would take with her and had given the rest to Molly. She'd also kept her mother's Bible and a few choice books.

Mr. Sloan nodded. "Will someone be coming to fetch you?"

"Yes." She did not want to tell him she'd be staying with a friend because she was now homeless.

Mr. Sloan looked past her. "I will direct the men to get started then."

Loretta had arranged with Clarissa to stay at her home for a few days until she could find permanent lodging. Clarissa and her husband would arrive in less than an hour to help Loretta with her meager belongings and to take her to their home. But in the time remaining, she would retrieve her mail.

The morning was gray and overcast as she walked

the two blocks to the post office. People were out and about, smiling and carrying on as though they didn't have a problem in the world. Oblivious to the pain she held in her own heart.

How she regretted taking for granted those days when everything had been going well! When she had a roof over her head and enough money to pay the bills.

She sighed. The fickleness of human existence struck her with full force. As the Good Book said, *Man is but a breath; his days are like a passing shadow.*

Her life was certainly like a shadow now. Not just a single shadow, but a life filled with shadows. Shadows around every corner.

Loretta reached the post office and climbed the steps to its entrance. She waited as an elderly woman made her way out of the building.

Loretta then entered and approached the counter. "Good morning, Henry." She greeted the postmaster and proceeded to Edward's post office box. It was filled with bills, bills, and more bills. Her heart clenched. How would she ever get back on her feet? Edward had left her in an absolute mess from which it seemed impossible ever to extricate herself. But, somehow, she would.

She had to.

As she sorted through the mail, she fought the recurrent anger that threatened to strangle her soul. Among the bills was a letter with a firm, square penmanship. She looked at the return address. Jeremiah Collins. Immediately she recognized the name. The owner of the fishing supply store.

Her muscles tightened. What could Mr. Collins possibly want? Especially after he'd practically thrown her out of his store?

She walked outside and sat on a bench in front of the post office. A few drops of rain now fell, threatening to burgeon into a full-blown downpour. She put the mail in her purse and hurried back to the house.

Once indoors, Loretta sat down on the sofa and opened the letter from Mr. Collins. It was dated Saturday, April 19, 1873, two days before.

My Dear Mrs. Vye,

I read your advertisement for a position in this morning's newspaper and am happy to reply with an offer. You visited my store last week in response to my Help Wanted *sign. At the time, I told you that I could not hire a woman. I have lived to regret my decision and would like to offer you both an apology and a job. As part of your salary, I can also extend the use of a small apartment on the second-floor of the building.*

If this offer interests you, please reply to me either by return letter or in person.

Sincerely,

Jeremiah Collins

P.S. I do hope you will accept my offer.

Loretta folded the letter. Should she be angry or grateful? Mr. Collins's original attitude of superiority had made it clear that he did not want a woman working in his store. If she accepted his offer, would she be conceding to his despicable prejudice? If she took the job, would he constantly lord it over her? Berate her? Humiliate her? Why should she subject herself to such treatment? She had at least a little self-respect left in her emotional arsenal.

At the same time, his offer would provide everything she needed. Income to get back on her feet plus a place to live while she did so. She'd be a fool not to accept it.

But she didn't want to do anything rash. Desperation often caused bad decisions. She took in a deep breath. She had less than an hour to make up her mind. Clarissa's carriage would be coming for her to take her to her friend's home. Should she request, instead, that she be taken to Mr. Collins's store?

Before responding, she would talk with Clarissa and ask her advice. Clarissa had been a wise mentor to her over the years and had always given Loretta wise counsel.

But something told her that Clarissa would advise her to take the job.

Monday, April 21

The clopping of horses' hooves in the near distance alerted Loretta to the approach of Clarissa's carriage. She rose, picked up the duffel bag containing her few remaining belongings, and descended the steps as the carriage rumbled to a halt at the curb.

"Good morning, Loretta." Clarissa greeted her from the front seat with a smile, as did her husband John. "John will help you with your bag."

Loretta hesitated. "I think I've had a change in plans."

"Oh?" Clarissa lifted a questioning brow.

"Shortly before you arrived, I retrieved my mail from the post office and found a most interesting letter."

"Do tell." Clarissa's wide eyes indicated eagerness for the news.

"The owner of Collins's Fishing Supply Store has reconsidered and offered me the job."

Her friend clapped her hands. "Thank the Lord. I'm so glad to hear that. This is truly a miracle from God. An answer to prayer."

"But not only a job. As part of the salary, he has offered me free occupancy of the apartment on the second floor above his store."

Clarissa grew pensive, as though weighing the pros and cons.

Loretta's concern rose a notch. "What do you think? Should I accept the offer?"

"I think you should."

"I think so too."

"That is quite a generous salary. And it seems to be a good way for you to get back on your feet." Clarissa nodded. "I would say, yes, accept the offer.'" She turned to her husband. "What do you think, John?"

"I agree. Jeremiah Collins is a fine man, a bit rough around the edges, but honest and fair."

Loretta's ears perked. "Oh, you know him?"

"Yes. My hobby is fishing for bluefish and flounder in the Delaware Bay, and I find all that I need to support that hobby at Jeremiah's store. I've been buying from him ever since he opened his store about three years ago."

Loretta's heart eased into a more settled rhythm. "I feel quite relieved knowing that." She paused. "In fact, instead of taking me to your home, would you mind driving me instead to the Collins Fishing Supply Store? I'd like to accept Mr. Collins's gracious offer in person. I'll then move my things directly into the apartment."

Clarissa nodded. "We can certainly do that, if it is your wish. Of course, know that you are more than welcome to stay with us until you are perfectly sure."

Resolve rose in Loretta's heart. "I'm perfectly sure." It was the right thing to do. Clarissa had been gracious to offer her a place to stay when Loretta had none, but now that the Lord had provided a place for her to live, she felt obliged to accept it.

"Very well, then." Clarissa smiled. "We shall redirect our course to Mr. Collins's Fishing Supply Store."

Loretta handed her bag to John and, with his help, mounted the carriage to the seat behind Clarissa's.

In a few moments, they reached the store.

Clarissa glanced back at Loretta. "We'll wait here until you finalize everything. I wouldn't want to leave you stranded if things don't work out as anticipated."

"Thank you. That's very kind of you." Dismounting the carriage with John's help, Loretta made her way up the steps to the entrance of Collins's Fishing Supply Store. Swallowing her pride, she walked up to the counter and waited for Mr. Collins to appear.

He came from the back room of the store and upon seeing her, his face broke into a warm smile. "You've come back." His voice was husky.

To her surprise, she was more drawn to him this second time around than the first. "Yes. Thank you for your letter. I've come back to accept your offer. It was a miraculous answer to prayer."

"Well, praise the Lord." He rubbed his chin. "I was worried you'd left town, and I would not be able to locate you."

As his face reddened, an awkward moment of silence passed between them.

Jeremiah cleared his throat. "I suppose I should show you to your quarters first and then, once you're settled, I'll explain the requirements of the job."

"Yes. That would be fine." Loretta motioned

toward the waiting carriage. “My things are outside. Some friends accompanied me.”

“I'll carry your bags in for you.”

“My bag.” She corrected him. “I have only one.” She then led him to Clarissa's carriage.

“Hello, Jeremiah.” John gave him a warm handshake.

“Well, if it isn't my old friend, John Steubens. What brings you to these parts?”

“My wife, Clarissa, and Loretta are longtime friends. We attend the same church, and Loretta is part of Clarissa's knitting circle.” John introduced Clarissa to Jeremiah.

She smiled. “Pleased to meet you, Mr. Collins.” She glanced at Loretta. “And thank you for offering my friend this opportunity.”

Jeremiah looked at Loretta. “Happy to help. Plus, she's helping me as well.”

Clarissa nodded toward Loretta. “You'll find Loretta to be an outstanding employee and a remarkable person.”

Loretta's heart warmed at Clarissa's endorsement. “Thank you, Clarissa.”

John removed Loretta's bag from the carriage and handed it to Jeremiah.

Clarissa descended from the carriage and gave

Loretta a warm hug. “May the Lord bless you as you begin this new phase of your life. Never forget that He is always with you and will never leave you nor forsake you.”

“Thank you, Clarissa. Your words mean a great deal to me.”

“You're welcome, my friend.”

Loretta took leave of Clarissa and John and followed Jeremiah into the new world of providing for herself. She entered it with both misgivings and expectancy.

Misgivings that she was not doing the right thing.

Expectancy that she was.

Monday, April 21, 1873

With Loretta's only bag in hand, Jeremiah led the way to the private side entrance to the second-floor apartment. His heart stirred with gratitude at the Lord's answer to his prayer. His heart also stirred with keen interest in the woman who followed him up the outside staircase.

When he reached the top, he withdrew a key from his shirt pocket, inserted it into the key hole, and unlocked the door. A strong, musty smell assaulted his nostrils. Had he known sooner of Loretta's arrival, he would have checked on the condition of the apartment.

He opened the door wide and allowed her to enter first. “I hope you like it. It's small but cozy.”

Loretta entered and looked around. A smile graced her face. “It will do quite well. Thank you.”

He quickly showed her around the three tiny rooms—a sitting room, a kitchen, a bedroom. Next to the bed stood a chamber pot and a washstand. An outhouse stood behind the building. “If there's anything you need, please let me know. Take your time getting organized. I will be downstairs in the store.”

Loretta smiled. “Thank you. I won't be long.”

Jeremiah descended the stairs, went outside, and re-entered the building through the front door. He went straight to the back room to prepare some coffee for both of them to sip while he explained Loretta’s duties.

His new female employee touched a deep place inside him. She was stunningly beautiful, charming, elegant, and all that he lacked. Having accepted the fact of a woman working in his employ, he was able to concentrate more on her good traits than on his chauvinism. Although, if he were honest, traces of that still remained.

But hiring her was the right thing to do. Moreover, it fed his sense of nobility in that he was helping a woman who, otherwise, might not be able to help herself.

Chapter Eleven

Monday, April 21, 1873

Loretta explored the tiny apartment, thanking God for providing it. The living room was warm and cozy, with a large window overlooking the main street. Two tufted chairs waited beside a small table with an oil lamp on it. A wood stove, with a stack of wood next to it, sat in one corner. Next to the wood stove was a bookshelf.

Loretta moved toward the kitchen. It held an icebox—a wonderful amenity—a small stove, and a pantry closet. Just enough for one person.

Next, she proceeded toward the bedroom, which held a narrow bed, an end table, and an oil lamp. On the wall hung a wooden Cross. Her heart relaxed in the knowledge that Jeremiah was an honorable man.

Loretta took a deep breath. She had everything she needed, and then some. Her heart overflowed with thanksgiving.

She took a moment to freshen up in front of a small mirror hanging on the bedroom wall. Then, taking the key with her, she locked the apartment door and headed downstairs to join Mr. Collins.

Monday, April 21, 1873

In a few moments, the bell over the door tinkled, indicating Mrs. Vye's arrival. Jeremiah hastened to the front of the store. He found her petting Burrows who had jumped on the counter to greet her.

His heart warmed. "So ... you like cats?"

She looked up and smiled. A smile that caused a lump to rise to his throat. "Yes. Cats and dogs. I used to have a calico cat and a Sheltie when I was a little girl."

"Well, I see Burrows likes you."

"How can you tell?"

"She usually takes her time warming up to strangers. The fact that she's allowing you to pet her is a sign that she trusts you."

"I'm glad." Loretta continued stroking the cat's soft fur.

Jeremiah's heart raced. From every angle, Mrs. Vye was a beauty. "Would you like a cup of coffee?"

She glanced at him, her deep-blue eyes awakening desire he'd long suppressed. "Actually, yes. I would appreciate that very much."

"Good. I'll get us two cups and then we can sit at the table by the window to talk."

Jeremiah went into the kitchen and poured two mugs of coffee. He put them on a small tray together with a pitcher of cream, a bowl of sugar, and two teaspoons. He then brought the tray out to the front of the store.

Loretta was already seated at the table with a happy Burrows on her lap. The sun streaming through the window highlighted the blond tints in her long, wavy hair. Jeremiah had difficulty taking his eyes off her and attending to business.

Tom Brogan was right. She was not a woman to let go. If Jeremiah didn't secure Loretta's heart, Tom would do his best to win it.

And Jeremiah would never allow that.

He swallowed the lump in his throat, placed her cup of coffee in front of her, and sat down in the chair across from hers. He struggled to calm his racing pulse. "Now, then, Mrs. Vye. Let me explain the duties and responsibilities that will be yours."

Loretta withdrew a note pad and a pencil from her reticule. "I'm ready." She gave him a smile that would melt the heart of any man.

Impressed by her diligence in wanting to take notes, Jeremiah began. "Your most important duty will be to show kindness and respect to our customers. They are the lifeblood of any business, and especially this one. Many of my customers have been with me since I first opened the store three years ago. John, for instance, is one of them. They are loyal, and their loyalty has provided a living for me. At the very least, I owe them my loyalty and faithfulness in return."

"Indeed. Kindness is the bedrock of any relationship, including business ones." She made a note in her notebook.

Jeremiah read the word *customers* in large letters on the page. "Next, I will show you how to enter purchases in the ledger and how to receive payment."

Loretta looked up, eagerness on her beautiful face.

Jeremiah's heart stirred. "It's really very easy, once

you've done it a couple of times." He pointed to the cash drawer. "Here, let me show you."

He rose, motioning her to follow him. As he stood by her side behind the counter, his heartbeat quickened. Her presence was palpable, in an unnerving, yet pleasant, way. As she drew closer to him, the fragrance of lavender ignited his senses.

Jeremiah cleared his throat as he first withdrew the ledger. "This is the book in which we record all sales. As you will note, there are several columns, each one labeled accordingly. For example, the first column lists the date; the second, the name of the item or items purchased; the third, the amount of sale, and the fourth, the running total of sales."

Loretta's gaze focused on the ledger.

"Now then, all you have to do after each sale is to fill in each column. But you will do this after the customer has paid you."

"How do I receive payment?"

Jeremiah smiled. "That's where the cash drawer comes in." He opened the top drawer of the cabinet under the counter. "This is the cash drawer. I keep the key on this little hook to the right of the cabinet. When the customer pays you, simply open the cash drawer and give him any necessary change. Also, please give him a receipt as well." Jeremiah showed her the pad of receipts kept inside the cash drawer. "You will notice that there is a sheet of carbon paper between each receipt. This will enable you to make a copy of the receipt for the customer and keep a copy for yourself."

"That looks easy enough."

"It is. But you must always remember to record sales at the end of the day in this ledger, using the carbon copies of the receipts." He pointed to a black book on the counter. "And that's all there is to it."

"I can do that."

'Of course, you can." A warm sensation came over him as he melted in the deep pools of her innocent eyes. "I will let you watch me handle the first few customers, and then I will let you do it." He hesitated. "I will be here, of course, until you gain confidence."

Loretta smiled, a look of deep gratitude in her eyes. "Thank you."

"Oh, one last thing. But, perhaps, the most important thing." He pointed to a cabinet beneath the cash register. "In there is a Colt revolver. Do you know how to fire one?"

Her eyes widened as she shook her head.

"Well, I'm going to teach you how. It's a required skill to hold a job here, especially for a woman."

He removed the gun from the cabinet and proceeded to explain its features. First, he showed her how to hold it. Next, he explained the trigger and how to work it. Then, he handed the gun to Loretta.

"Now, you try it. I'll stand beside you to guide you."

Giving him a nervous glance, Loretta tightened her grip on the revolver.

Jeremiah stood next to her and placed his hand on hers. A powerful desire to embrace her rushed through him. He backed away, catching his breath. "Perhaps we should plan a practice session soon."

Loretta nodded, her face a lovely shade of crimson.

Jeremiah put away the gun. "You never know when you'll need to protect yourself, especially when I'm not here."

The bell tinkled above the door as Tom Brogan entered and closed the door behind him. A broad smile spread across his face when he saw Loretta. "Well, Jeremiah my friend, I see you hired the perty lady."

Jeremiah stiffened at the suggestive look Tom gave Loretta. "Yes, I did."

Tom walked up to Loretta and extended a welcoming hand. "I'm Tom Brogan, a friend of Jeremiah." Tom's leering gaze scanned Loretta from head to toe.

Jeremiah's jealousy exploded within him. Tom was a little too friendly with Loretta. Jeremiah moved a bit closer to her and placed a hand on her shoulder. "I'm right proud to have Mrs. Vye working for me."

Tom nodded. "Yes, I think she'll do wonders for your business."

Jeremiah read between the lines. Word that a beauty like Loretta worked in his store would get around quickly, attracting the available men in the community. And, sad to say, perhaps even the unavailable ones.

He'd better establish boundaries sooner rather than later.

Especially with Tom Brogan.

Wednesday, May 14, 1873

Nearly a month had transpired since Loretta had started working at the fishing supply store. Each day, she'd found herself growing increasingly fond of Jeremiah. His very presence stirred feelings in her she'd never felt before. Not even when married to Edward. She was drawn to Jeremiah in a way she hadn't been to Edward.

The night before, she'd decided to surprise him by

baking strawberry scones, his favorite dessert. She'd give them to him today.

As she busied herself straightening some items on the shelves, he entered the room. "Good morning, Loretta."

"Good morning." She gave him a warm smile. "Have you had your coffee yet?"

"No. Would you like a cup?"

"That sounds wonderful. It would go well with a little treat I made for you."

His eyes widened. "A treat?"

"Yes." She walked to the cabinet behind the counter and retrieved the plate of scones. "I baked these for you."

His gaze locked onto hers. "For me?" He was visibly moved.

"Yes. You've been so kind to me that I had to do something in return." She put the scones on the table while he went to get the coffee.

Jeremiah returned and placed a mug of steaming coffee in front of her. "You are quite an amazing woman."

"And you're quite an amazing man." She wanted to take his hand and hold it in hers, but propriety would not permit it.

They talked for a good half hour. About her late

husband Edward. About his late wife Anna Mae and the child they'd lost. About his dreams for his business. And about her desire to open a knitting shop one day. By the time they'd finished, Loretta had fallen head over heels in love with Jeremiah Collins.

The only problem was that he didn't seem to reciprocate her feelings.

Chapter Twelve

Monday, June 16, 1873

By the time June rolled around, Loretta had developed a routine and had grown accustomed to dealing with the rough, gruff fishermen who frequented the establishment. Thus far, her firm words had been sufficient to stave off any ill-mannered man. The gun remained in its place. No matter that she hadn't yet learned how to use it.

Jeremiah brought the ledger from the back of the store for her to see. "Business has doubled since you've started working for me."

She smiled, stifling a surge of pride. "That makes

me happy. I was worried that I would hurt your business rather than help it."

Jeremiah chuckled. "Well, it seems that every man likes a pretty woman."

Loretta tensed. "I hope I'm attracting customers because of my competence and not because of my looks."

Jeremiah hesitated. "I wish I could say that was the case. But most of the compliments I've received had to do with your looks."

Loretta's stomach clenched. If she could, she'd quit right on the spot. Being appreciated for her looks alone was insulting. Condescending. Chauvinistic. "So you're saying that no one has complimented me for my abilities?"

Jeremiah shook his head. "I'm afraid not." He paused and looked her in the eye. "Although, I must say, *I've* been quite impressed with your competence. You've exceeded my wildest expectations."

Her heart warmed at his assessment of her skills. But she couldn't let the matter of her looks go. "Has anything at all been said about my competence?"

Jeremiah rubbed his neck. "Only that it—occasionally—seems wanting."

Loretta's belly filled with fire. "Wanting? In what way?'

Jeremiah's face twisted. "Truth be told, Loretta, I've gotten several comments from customers who claim not to receive suitable answers to their questions. It's quite obvious that you are not familiar with the fishing industry."

Loretta placed her hands on her hips. "Why didn't you tell me sooner instead of allowing me to make a fool of myself?"

"You haven't made a fool of yourself." He raked his fingers through his hair. "You've simply demonstrated that you need to learn more about the industry."

"Then teach me more!" Frustration edged her voice. Why hadn't Jeremiah spoken to her about the customers' reactions? Why hadn't he pointed out her areas of weakness?

"Very well. We'll start today, after closing hours. We'll spend thirty minutes a day going from shelf to shelf. I will explain each product and its use." His gaze locked on hers. "And, remember ... you can always ask me for advice when you have a question."

She raised her voice a decibel. "But I haven't had a question because I didn't know there was a question to be had."

He laughed. "My dear Loretta—"

"I am not *your* dear Loretta." She placed her hands on her hips. "I am your furious Loretta."

Jeremiah chuckled. “Well, at least you're *my* Loretta.”

Her ire flared. “How dare you say such a thing?”

He winked. “It was you who agreed by saying ‘I am *your* furious Loretta.’”

She lowered her hands and huffed.

He grew serious. “I’m sorry. I meant no disrespect.”

What did he mean then? Did he mean he felt something for her? That same something for him that was growing inside of her? That she was afraid of revealing to him?

She brushed the front of her skirt. “I suppose I should get back to work.”

“I need to run an errand and will be back in an hour. Do you think you can handle the store alone?”

So he truly did trust her. “I'm sure I can.”

But what she couldn't handle was the longing for Jeremiah that was growing in the depths of her heart.

* * *

Monday, June 16, 1873

. . .

Shortly after Jeremiah left, Tom Brogan sauntered into the store. "Well, well, well. If it ain't the perty Lady Loretta." His breath reeked of alcohol.

Loretta tensed. "Good day, Mr. Brogan." She maintained her composure while keeping her distance. "How may I help you today?"

He gave her a leering smirk and approached the counter. "Do ya really wanna know?"

She grabbed the countertop, inches from the handgun. "Mr. Brogan, I must ask you to leave. It is quite obvious that you are inebriated. I think it best that you go home, sleep it off, and then return when Jeremiah is here."

He placed both palms on the counter, his alcoholic breath right in her face. "I don't wanna go home." He slurred his words. "I wanna stay right here with you. I came to get what's mine. That ole Jeremiah thinks he can steal you from me, does he? Well, I'll show him a thing or two."

She backed away, still holding the countertop. "Mr. Brogan, you don't know what you're saying. I insist you leave immediately or—"

He laughed derisively. "Or what? Do you think a little woman like you can overpower a big man like me?"

Panic gripped her. She grabbed the gun and

pointed it at him. She must not let him know she feared him.

He scoffed. "You know no more about shootin' a pistol than you do about sellin' fishin' supplies."

"If you come any closer, I'll shoot."

He took a step closer.

She cocked the hammer. She had to run him out of the store or hold him at bay until Jeremiah returned, whichever came first.

He took another step toward her.

"I warn you, Mr. Brogan. You will not leave here alive if you come one step closer."

"You wouldn't dare shoot me."

"I most certainly would." Loretta kept the gun pointed at him. "Now leave this instant."

Suddenly, Burrows jumped up on the counter and hissed at Tom.

He backed away. "Get that stupid cat outa here!"

In a flash, Burrows leapt toward Tom and clawed his face before dropping to the floor.

He screamed in pain. "You'll pay for this, Loretta Vye! And so will that lover of yours!" In an instant, he was out the door, clutching his wounded face.

Loretta locked the door and collapsed into the chair, her body trembling all over.

At the sound of a knock on the door several

minutes later, she startled. When she looked up, Jeremiah stood outside, trying to get in.

She rose and unlocked the door, the pistol still in her hand. "I'm sorry. I had to lock the door."

Jeremiah looked down at the pistol. "What happened?" He entered and closed the door behind him.

"Tom Brogan was here." Her breath was shallow and her voice quaked. "He was drunk. He threatened to assault me." She gasped for air. "He said you tried to steal me from him."

Jeremiah's arm came around her shoulders. "Come. Sit down." He led her to the chair. "I'll get you a glass of water." Before he went to the back room, he locked the front door again.

When Jeremiah came back with the water, she recounted the entire incident to him, including Tom's threat. Was it an empty one? Or did Tom Brogan mean what he said?

Jeremiah looked out the window. "I don't want that man ever stepping foot in my store again."

Loretta nodded. "Neither do I." From now on, she would do everything in her power to avoid Tom Brogan.

But how?

* * *

Monday, June 16, 1873

Jeremiah sat at his kitchen table that evening, head in his hands. His appetite was gone. He'd forced himself to eat a bowl of vegetable soup, only to keep up his strength. But the food became a dead weight in his stomach.

Tom Brogan's attempted attack on Loretta earlier that day had shaken him unlike anything had before. Never in his wildest imagination would he have thought that Tom would do such a thing, especially since he called himself Jeremiah's friend.

Yes, Tom drank a little too much at times, but he'd always seemed to be able to control his liquor. But his appearance in the store today in a drunken condition had been an outrage. Loretta could have been seriously hurt. Maybe even killed.

And Jeremiah would have been responsible.

He shuddered at the thought.

The incident haunted his mind. It was all he'd been able to think about all afternoon.

Jeremiah shook his head in disbelief. His insides roiled as he stood and placed his empty bowl in the sink. He must no longer leave Loretta alone in the store. He knew Tom well enough to know that his outbursts of anger were nothing to take lightly. More than once, the man had beaten up another man at the local saloon. But a woman! Tom would never dare assault a woman.

Yet that's precisely what he'd attempted to do that very day. And in Jeremiah's own store. The brazenness of it all!

Jeremiah swallowed the bile that rose from his belly. His mama's words surfaced to his mind. *People are not always what they appear to be.* Well, Mama's statement was certainly true about Tom Brogan. Much to Jeremiah's dismay, the man had fooled him. But, how did the saying go? *Fool me once, shame on you; fool me twice, shame on me.* No. No matter what he had to do, Jeremiah would never allow Tom Brogan to fool him again.

Most of all, Jeremiah would never allow him to come near Loretta again.

He sat back down. Burrows jumped onto his lap. Jeremiah stroked her soft fur as his mind raced to make plans to keep Loretta safe.

What was he thinking in leaving Loretta alone in an environment that exposed her to lustful, foul-mouthed men? While most of his customers knew how to act in the presence of a lady, there were always those few bravados who spoke loosely, with no compunction for their brashness, let alone any respect for a woman. This was one of the reasons Jeremiah had not wanted to hire Loretta in the first place. She was too delicate a flower to be exposed to such men. Too innocent to be even in their presence for an instant.

Too precious not to be his wife.

His soul jolted. Where had that thought come from? A lump formed in his throat. Truth be told, he'd been pondering it in the secret recesses of his heart for a while now. But, until now, he'd been afraid to admit it, even to himself. In the two months since Loretta had started working for him, he'd grown fond of her. More than fond. He'd fallen in love with her.

She'd stirred within him a longing for that woman's touch Tom had spoken of. That part of life that a man lacked and felt incomplete without. That other half of man which only woman was.

Jeremiah stiffened. That's what Tom Brogan was after. That woman's touch. But Tom's desire for Loretta was unholy. Lustful. Selfish. And, therefore, forbidden.

It was up to Jeremiah to protect her from Tom, and from every other man who tried to harm her in any way. But how could he best do that?

His breath caught. Only by marrying her.

Even wicked men thought twice before touching another man's wife. As long as Loretta remained unmarried, she was fair game, a prime target for men with evil intent.

But would Loretta have him? She'd never shown any sign of interest in him other than that of employee to employer. She'd never expressed the least indication that she felt for him the way he felt for her.

But, then again, had he ever given her any indication of his affection for her? He had not. He'd been too afraid. Afraid she'd reject him. Afraid she'd deem him unworthy of her. Afraid she didn't need him.

Therefore, he'd done what he could. He'd provided her with a job whereby she could take care of herself.

But now, she needed more from him. She needed absolute protection while she worked. So, that's what he would give her.

Until he found the courage to give her more.

First, he'd make sure she was never alone in the store again. But doing so posed several problems. First of all, he had business errands to run throughout the week. Times when he had to be away from the store. He couldn't afford to diminish the number of hours he was open. Doing so would hurt business. If only he were in a financial position to hire another employee to work with her. But that was out of the question.

The only option that remained to him–and it was a painful one—was to let Loretta go and to hire a man in her place. It would be for her own good. Her own safety. He couldn't risk her being hurt. Not only because she was a woman. He swallowed hard. But because she was Loretta.

But he wouldn’t let her go until he helped her secure another position.

He stroked the cat still on his lap. “This is going to be a tough one, Burrows. What decision should I make?”

To his surprise, Burrows hunched her back, looked up at him, and hissed.

Jeremiah chuckled. “Thanks for your opinion.”

Burrows knew him well. Jeremiah loved Loretta too much to let her go.

Chapter Thirteen

Tuesday, June 17, 1873

An acrid smell awakened Loretta in the middle of the night. Startled, she rose from her bed to find her little apartment filled with smoke. Coughing her way to the window, she opened it for air only to discover flames licking the lower side of the building.

Panic gripped her heart. She must awaken Jeremiah.

She grabbed her robe and ran out of the apartment, down the outside stairway. By God's grace, the stairway was still intact. Flames licked against it as she rushed down, barely tripping over her robe. Fear thundered within her.

As she reached the front door, Loretta's heart sank. She'd forgotten to bring her key. What to do now? Not a soul was around at this time of night. If she ran to get help, the entire building would be destroyed before her return.

Pounding on the front door with all her might, she shouted Jeremiah's name. But there was no response. Had he been overcome with smoke? Terror snaked through her heart, threatening to strangle it. She could not let him die. She would not let him die.

She searched around for something with which to break into the store. She grabbed a large rock lying on the ground and threw it through the front door window, shattering it and enabling her to reach in and unlock the door. As she opened it, Burrows escaped to the outside.

Once inside, Loretta ran to the back room where Jeremiah lay on his bed.

"Jeremiah! Jeremiah!" She shook him forcefully, but he did not respond. Was he dead or alive?

Without waiting to find out, she lowered herself to his side, pulled his arms over her shoulders, and lifted him out of the bed. Pressing the weight of his body against her back, she opened the back door with one hand and dragged him out and away from the building.

Her pulse raced. There was no time to lose. The flames now encroached upon the perimeter of the backyard, eating up the dry grass and bushes. She muttered a quick prayer for strength and safety, hoping that her bathrobe would not catch hold of the flames.

When she was far enough away from the burning building, she gently lowered Jeremiah to the ground, catching her breath as she did so.

She checked for his pulse but could not find it. Loretta gently slapped his cheeks to restore him to consciousness, but he did not respond. She placed her ear against his chest and let out a sigh of relief. Thank God. Shallow breathing.

By this time, neighbors had noticed the fire and had called for help. The piercing wail of a siren signaled an approaching fire truck.

In a moment, the fire brigade appeared carrying buckets of water.

She ran toward one of the firefighters. "Please! Please help!"

"Lady, get out of the way! You could get yourself killed!"

"Please. A man is dying. He needs a doctor right away."

The firefighter glanced between her and the

conflagration, his heavy brows meeting in the middle. "Let me get help. Better to save a life than a building."

Loretta ran ahead, knelt by Jeremiah's side, and took his hand. Tears coursed down her cheeks. *O God, please let him live. Please let him live.* Whatever she did, she had to keep him alive. Her heart clenched. She *needed* to keep him alive.

In a moment, the firefighter returned with another man.

"Hurry! He's fading." Loretta's breath caught.

"We'll get him to the hospital." The two men carefully lifted Jeremiah, one supporting his head and back, the other his legs.

Loretta followed close behind as they took Jeremiah to a waiting ambulance. As they placed him inside, the agitated horses neighed.

In an instant, the ambulance was gone, leaving Loretta alone by the side of the road. She turned toward the burning building as it collapsed in flames. Not only had she lost her home and her job, but she could lose Jeremiah as well.

Her heart clenched at the unbearable thought.

She swallowed hard. What would they do now? The dear man had lost his only means of livelihood. What would *she* do now? Her future had gone up in flames. Only the clothes on her back remained. Could matters get any worse?

She blinked back the stinging tears. She wanted to die. But she had to live. If not for her sake, for the sake of the man whom she was growing to love more and more each day.

Wednesday, June 18, 1873

When the firefighters had finished dousing the blaze, they took Loretta to Clarissa's house. Her dear friend welcomed her warmly, gave her shelter for the night, and provided her with fresh clothing.

The next morning, Loretta, overcome with exhaustion, sat with Clarissa in her friend's kitchen. The sun shone brightly through the large window over the sink.

Clarissa poured coffee into Loretta's cup. "Have you seen the morning newspaper?"

"No. Why do you ask?" Loretta took a sip of her coffee.

Clarissa reached for the newspaper on the countertop and handed it to Loretta.

Loretta read the headlines. *Arson Suspected in*

Fishing Store Fire. Her heart nearly stopped. Was this true? If so, who would want to burn down Jeremiah's store? Who carried such a vendetta against him as to destroy his livelihood—and his life? If the allegation were true, the situation was worse than she'd thought.

Loretta continued reading. Apparently, around midnight the night before, a passerby had noticed a man trespassing on Jeremiah's property and carrying an oil can. The passerby had thought nothing of it. But, later, upon learning of the fire, he'd made the possible connection and had reported the incident to the police.

Loretta laid the paper on her lap and stared in shock at Clarissa.

Clarissa placed a hand on Loretta's arm. "Who would want to destroy a good man like Jeremiah Collins?"

"Tom Brogan." The name slid slowly from Loretta's lips. Hadn't he threatened vengeance upon her when she'd refused his advances? Hadn't he threatened to destroy Jeremiah as well?

Clarissa's eyes widened. "But, he's Jeremiah's friend."

"And Judas was Jesus's friend."

Loretta recounted to Clarissa the incident of Tom's threatened assault upon her while she was alone minding the store. Of Tom's foolish belief that Jeremiah had stolen her from him. And of his threat to destroy them both.

Clarissa gasped. “Thank God, he didn't harm you.”

“Oh, Clarissa.” Loretta’s voice choked. “I was the instigating factor in the fire. I know I was. Tom was angry with me, so he took it out on Jeremiah.”

Clarissa looked straight at Loretta. “Now, don't go blaming yourself. You are not responsible for Tom's actions. He was jealous and acted out of that jealousy.”

Loretta rose and paced the kitchen. “Regardless, if it weren't for me, Tom would have had nothing to be jealous about.” Loretta's eyes welled up with tears.

“But, Loretta, you can't be sure it was Tom who perpetrated this horrendous crime. Before you blame yourself, or him, get all the facts.”

Loretta sat down again. “I know it was Tom. But, as you said, there is no tangible proof.”

“I suggest you put the matter into the Lord's hands, and let Him work it out. If Tom is guilty, the Lord will expose it.”

Loretta lowered her head. “I know you're right. I need to cast this care on the Lord. It's just that I'm sick over the possibility that I am the cause of Jeremiah's destruction.”

Clarissa's voice grew firm. "Loretta, you must not blame yourself for something that was not your fault. Tom Brogan has a free will, and if he's guilty, he chose to use it for evil."

"But, still ... this would never have happened had I not been the catalyst." Loretta wrung her hands. "I need to visit Jeremiah at the hospital and tell him that I think the arsonist is Tom Brogan."

"Very well. But whatever else you do, do not spread that allegation until the facts prove it true."

Tuesday, June 17, 1873

Loretta thanked Clarissa for her wise advice and headed to the hospital. She found Jeremiah sitting up in bed.

Her heart soared upon seeing him. "Good morning, Jeremiah. You look much improved over last night."

He took her hand. "Thank you for saving my life."

If only she could tell him that she would have given her very own life to save his. "It was the grace of God that saved both of us."

He squeezed his eyes shut. "Yes, you're right."

Loretta drew a chair up to the bedside and sat down. "Jeremiah, there is something I must tell you."

His eyes were glued to her. "What is it, my dear Loretta?"

She did not miss his choice of words. Could it be he held her in as high esteem as she held him? "After you were taken to the hospital last night, and after the fire was completely extinguished, the firefighters took me to Clarissa's home. I spent the remainder of the night there. She fed me and gave me a fresh set of clothes."

"That was very kind of her."

"She also showed me the morning newspaper." She hesitated. "The headlines show a strong suspicion of arson as the cause of the fire."

Jeremiah's face paled. "Arson?"

"Yes. Arson. When I first read it, it seemed as incredible to me as it must to you."

"But who would want to burn down my store? And for what reason?"

"I think it was Tom Brogan."

Jeremiah gaped at her. "Tom? How can that be?"

"Jeremiah, Tom attempted to assault me. When I refused his advances, he threatened to take vengeance on both of us."

Jeremiah raked his fingers through his hair. “I am stunned to say the least.” His gaze skittered back to her. “But we have no proof.”

Loretta lowered her voice. “That's true.” She hesitated. “I've never liked Tom Brogan from the first moment I met him. There's something sinister about him. He is not what he seems to be.”

Just then a nurse walked into the room. “There's a gentleman to see you, sir. He says his name is Tom Brogan. Are you up for another visitor?”

Loretta shot a warning glance at Jeremiah.

“Let him in, please.”

In a few moments, Tom entered the room and stood at the foot of the bed. “Jeremiah old boy, so sorry to hear about the fire.”

Loretta's stomach clenched.

Tom turned toward Loretta. “I'm surprised to see you here, Mrs. Vye.” He gave her the familiar, leering look.

Jeremiah was quick to explain. “It was Mrs. Vye who saved my life.”

Tom's eyebrow shot up. “Really? That's quite a feat for a petite woman like Mrs. Vye.”

Loretta stiffened. “Women are quite capable of doing more than what men give them credit for, Mr. Brogan.” It felt good to put Tom in his place.

Tom scowled. "I see we have a feisty woman on our hands, Jeremiah. I find that quite attractive, don't you?"

"I would prefer to call her strong. No other woman alive would have risked her life to save mine."

Tom smirked. "Then, it's obvious that Mrs. Vye cares deeply for you."

Heat flooded Loretta's face. "That is none of your business, Mr. Brogan. Furthermore, I assume that you came to visit Jeremiah, not to discuss the personal matters of my heart."

An angry look crossed Tom's face. "My apologies, Mrs. Vye." He moved to the side of the bed opposite Loretta. "So, how are you doin', my friend?"

"Thankful to be alive. I could have died from the smoke inhalation. Few survive such an ordeal."

"The Almighty's face must've been shinin' on you." Tom crossed his arms. "Any idea who started the fire?"

Loretta shot a glance at Jeremiah. Her muscles tightened. "You know of the allegation of arson?"

His face paled. "I read of it in this mornin's newspaper."

Jeremiah's eyes narrowed. "I have no known enemy who would want to destroy me and my livelihood. Especially in such a horrendous way."

Tom squared his jaw. "Well, then, the arsonist remains to be identified, I see." He paused. "If there is anything I can do to help in the investigation, please let me know."

You can tell us the truth, Tom Brogan! The thought flew into Loretta's mind. Once again, her gut told her something wasn't right. While she never wanted falsely to accuse anyone of wrongdoing, somehow Tom's offer to help seemed like an attempt to distract and divert attention from himself as the culprit.

"I will." Jeremiah thanked Tom for his offer.

"Well, I best be goin'." Tom reached for Jeremiah's hand and shook it. He turned toward Loretta. "Good day, Mrs. Vye."

She stood, unwilling to sit under his discomfiting gaze. "Good day, Mr. Brogan."

He gave her a slight bow and then left, leaving a trail of unanswered questions in his wake.

Chapter Fourteen

Thursday, June 19, 1873

After Tom left the hospital room, Loretta addressed Jeremiah. “I don't trust that man.”

“Why not?”

She shifted in her chair. “After what he did, why would I?”She stood and paced the room. “I have no logical reason to believe this, but my womanly intuition tells me that Tom Brogan is the arsonist.”

“Well, there's not much I can do about it while confined to this hospital bed. But as soon as I'm discharged, I will investigate until I get some answers. Meanwhile, the police are working on the matter as well.”

Loretta approached Jeremiah's bedside. "The most important thing you can do now is to get better." Without thinking, she placed a hand on his. Lightning coursed through her veins, and she quickly withdrew her hand.

Jeremiah watched her, a strange look in his eyes. "Thank you for saving my life, Loretta. Had I been alone, I would surely have perished."

A lump formed in her throat. "You would have done the same for me."

"Absolutely." His gaze lingered on her for a long moment, sending warmth throughout her body. "Now that we've lost the building, I want to help you find a place to live."

She cleared her throat. "I'll stay with Clarissa for the time being, until I figure out what to do next."

"I suppose you will be looking for another job as well."

She lowered her eyes and raised them again. "Yes. My cousin Lil in Atlanta has been wanting me to come work in her restaurant. I had told her that I had already committed to working for you. But now, I may just take her up on her offer."

His face saddened. "I will hate to see you go, Loretta." He hesitated. "But I certainly understand. I have no idea what my insurance company will give me in damages. I hope it's enough for me to start over."

"I hope so too." Her heart ached for this man who had given her hope when she'd had no hope. If only she could offer him the same hope now that the tables were turned. If only she could tell him how she felt about him. But he'd never given her any reason to think he had any comparable feelings for her. To him, she was nothing more than a good friend. An employee. "What about you? Where will you live?"

"I plan to rent a room at the boardinghouse in the center of town. I'll stay there until I've rebuilt my building or have found another location for my store."

"I will pray for you, Jeremiah."

He studied her. "Thank you. And I, for you."

The nurse walked in. "I'm sorry to interrupt, ma'am, but visiting hours are over. The patient needs some rest."

"Yes, of course."

Loretta took one last look at Jeremiah, his eyes heavy with sleep. Leaving him was like wrenching a finger from a hand.

But leaving him was something she had to do.

Thursday, June 19, 1873

After visiting Jeremiah, Loretta reached Clarissa's house just as her friend was exiting the front door.

Upon seeing her, Clarissa stopped short. "I'm headed to the knitting circle meeting. Are you up to joining us today?" She put an arm around Loretta's shoulder.

"Frankly, I'm quite exhausted. I need to get some sleep."

"Of course, my dear. I shall see you upon my return then."

Loretta went to her room and collapsed on the bed. In short order, she was fast asleep.

She awakened from her nap shortly before Clarissa returned. When she went downstairs, she found her friend in the kitchen preparing lunch.

"Why, hello!" Clarissa smiled. "Did you get some good sleep?"

"Yes. Thank God."

"Come, let's have a cup of tea while you tell me about your visit with Jeremiah. How is he?"

Heat rose to Loretta's face. "He's doing much better. He's rented a room at a boardinghouse downtown. He hopes the insurance company will pay him for damages so that he can start over again."

"He's welcome to stay with us, you know."

"I know. You and John are so kind."

Clarissa looked at her a long moment and then smiled. "You've taken a shine to Jeremiah, haven't you?"

Loretta's cheeks burned. "What makes you say that?"

"I see the spark in your eyes when you speak of him."

"Don't be silly, Clarissa. Jeremiah is nothing but a friend. A good friend who helped me out in my time of need."

Clarissa did not look convinced. "The heart is deceitful above all things." She gave Loretta a knowing smile as she quoted the familiar Scripture verse from the book of Jeremiah. "What are you going to do now that you no longer have a job?"

Loretta tensed. "I haven't had much time to think about that. I suppose I'll move to Georgia to work for my cousin. She has a small restaurant and could use some help. She'd invited me to work for her earlier, but I had already taken the job with Jeremiah."

Clarissa nodded. "By the way, the ladies missed you

this morning. Ornella announced that she is with child again."

"What wonderful news! This is her fourth, right?"

"Yes." Clarissa's eyes lit up. "And our dear Cholena traveled up the road to attend a camp meeting at the Cape May County Fairgrounds this past weekend and met a man who tickled her fancy."

"You don't say?" Loretta giggled. "He must be quite the man to attract Cholena's attention. When it comes to men, she's not easy to please."

"I must admit, I've never seen her so happy."

The front door opened as Clarissa's husband John entered. He whiffed the air. "I smell something good cooking."

Clarissa rose to greet him with a peck on the cheek. "You're just in time. I made some homemade chicken soup."

John put his hat on the hat rack by the door and greeted Loretta. "Any word on Jeremiah?"

"Yes. I saw him this morning, and he's much better, thank God."

John smiled. "Glad to hear that. I must stop by to see him and to ask how I can help."He pulled out a chair and sat down.

Clarissa brought three bowls of piping-hot, homemade chicken soup to the table, and then John gave the blessing over the food.

Loretta took a spoonful. "Jeremiah will be staying at a boardinghouse in town until he's well."

John put down his spoon. "Nonsense! I insist that he stay here with us."

Clarissa chimed in. "That's precisely what I said, John."

Loretta's heart overflowed with gratitude. God had provided her with friends who were closer than her own family. "Thank you both so very much. But I think Jeremiah will have to make that decision."

John chuckled. "With a little bit of prodding from his old friend John, I don't think that decision will be too difficult for him to make."

After they finished the meal, Clarissa rose to clear the table. "Loretta, I'll bring up an extra set of towels. If there's anything else you need, please let me know."

"Thank you. I plan to write to my cousin this afternoon to inquire about the position at her restaurant. If she still has one for me, I'll be off to Georgia as soon as possible." Loretta paused. "If Jeremiah agrees to stay with you, I will leave in peace."

"And if not?" Clarissa gave her a questioning look.

But Loretta preferred not to answer that question.

* * *

Thursday evening, June 19, 1873

When Jeremiah awakened, it was already evening. He'd slept most of the day. A good sign, as was his returning appetite. He glanced at the wall clock. Six o'clock. The night nurse would soon be in with his evening meal.

His mind revisited the events surrounding the fire. With it had come not only the destruction of his livelihood, but also the destruction of his dream. The fishing store had been his promise of a future. A future that, lately, had included the thought of proposing marriage to Loretta.

Unbeknownst to her, he'd found himself captivated not only by her beauty, but most of all, by her kindness, her faithfulness, and her gentle spirit—so much so that he'd fallen in love with her. She'd become a fixture in the fishing supply store and, for the most part, had been well-received by his clientèle. To his great relief. Of course, there were those men who still didn't like the idea of a woman working in such a trade. But, on the whole, Loretta had been an asset to his business rather than a liability.

But now, she'd become far more than a business

asset. She'd become a personal necessity to him. Indeed, he could no longer imagine life without her. Learning that she'd be leaving Cape May for better pastures broke his heart. But why should she stay? He had nothing left to offer her–absolutely nothing—even if she would accept his proposal of marriage. It would take years for him to recover his footing. His meager savings were not enough to support a wife, let alone to support himself.

The night-duty nurse interrupted his thoughts. "Here's your dinner, Mr. Collins." She placed the tray on the little table next to the bed. "Now, I expect you to eat all of it, do you hear?" The twinkle in her eye told him she was only half serious.

"I'll do my best." He sat up in bed. "But you have to admit that hospital food leaves something to be desired."

She quirked her mouth. "We make it bland on purpose, so that our patients are motivated to recover, leave, and get back to delicious, home-cooked meals."

Jeremiah laughed. "So the secret is out."

The nurse waved a dismissive hand at him. "Now, eat." In a moment, she was off to her next patient.

As Jeremiah closed his eyes to thank the Lord for his food, he added a special request. "And, Lord, if it be

Your will that I marry Loretta Vye, please make a way where there seems to be no way. In Your Name, I pray. Amen."

Chapter Fifteen

Friday, June 20, 1873

The next morning, Loretta counted her remaining money. It was just enough to purchase a one-way ticket to Atlanta. As soon as she received a reply from her cousin, she would secure the ticket. With the few cents left over, she'd buy some necessary items for her trip.

Notifying Clarissa that she was going out, Loretta made her way to the Cape May General Store. The day was lovely, with a cloudless blue sky and a gentle breeze coming inland from the ocean. Along the way, children laughed as they played hide-and-seek. Mothers carried baskets of clean laundry recently removed from clotheslines.

At last, Loretta arrived at the general store. Several customers browsed the many shelves of items, greeting one another with a smile. While walking down the toiletries aisle, Loretta overheard a woman mention her name. Loretta stopped to listen.

The woman's voice was low. "If only Jeremiah Collins had known what a slut that Loretta Vye is, he would have never hired her. She looks with lustful eyes at nearly every man who comes into that store. Why, I went to Jeremiah's once with my husband, and she even tried to seduce him."

Loretta's heart stopped as the devastating bullet pierced her soul, sucking the very breath out of her lungs. Her head began to spin. She grabbed the nearest shelf to keep herself from falling and leaned her trembling frame against it.

"Of all atrocities!" The other woman chimed in. "Why, Tom Brogan himself said she tried to seduce him, but he resisted her advances. Imagine that! Tom Brogan of all people. Tom's a good man if I ever saw one. Wouldn't hurt a fly, although he does get a bit heavy with his liquor every once in a while."

"Well," the first woman continued, "all I know is that Cape May don't need the likes of Loretta Vye roamin' our streets. This here's a family town, and we aim to keep it that way."

Loretta could take no more. Leaving her basket of items on the shelf, she ran out of the store into the afternoon rain. Fortunately, the rain mingled with her tears so that when she reached Clarissa's house, she wouldn't have to explain why she was crying.

Her mind was made up. She'd leave on the next train, before the evil gossip got back to Jeremiah and ruined his reputation. She'd already caused him trouble enough as it was, what with instigating the fire. Once Tom Brogan's vicious and smearing accusation got back to him—and it would in no time—Jeremiah would want nothing more to do with her.

Friday, June 20, 1873

Without waiting for a reply from her cousin, Loretta packed for Georgia that very afternoon. Cousin Lil lived in the center of downtown Atlanta, in a small, two-bedroom apartment above her restaurant. If Loretta took the evening train, she'd arrive just before noon the next morning.

She informed Clarissa of her imminent departure without divulging the vicious gossip about herself she'd heard in the general store. It was too painful to share even with her treasured mentor. Besides, Clarissa would find out soon enough. The gossip would spread quickly. And not only spread quickly, but be embellished along the way.

Loretta also asked Clarissa to give Jeremiah her warmest regards and thanks. She hoped to see him again one day, if the Lord willed.

"Jeremiah will be devastated when he learns of your sudden departure. I will go with John to the boardinghouse to notify him after Jeremiah is discharged from the hospital. Meanwhile, may we take you to the train station?"

"Thank you, but there's no need. It's a short walk, and I have only one bag to take with me."

"Very well, my dear. I shall be praying for safe travel and good things upon your arrival."

"Thank you." Tears welled up in Loretta's eyes. "You've been a loyal friend to me, Clarissa. I shall sorely miss you."

"And I, you." Clarissa's eyes glistened. "God go with you, dear one." She gave Loretta a tight hug.

With heavy heart, Loretta walked to the train station and boarded the six o'clock train for Atlanta, due to arrive the following morning around ten.

Clarissa had given her a little bag of fruit and some apple cakes to eat along the way.

The train left right on time and traveled throughout the night. Except for stops in Washington, DC, and Richmond, Virginia, it lumbered onward toward Atlanta. Loretta sat on the wooden bench, unable to sleep. Three other passengers shared the cabin with her—a man, a woman, and an infant. The poor child cried most of the night, whether of fear or cholic, Loretta could not tell. By the time the train arrived in Atlanta, she was utterly exhausted.

Upon descending the train, Loretta found an empty bench in the bustling station and sat down. She'd saved the last apple cake for her breakfast this morning. Once she'd finished eating it, she went up to the ticket agent to ask for directions to her cousin's restaurant.

The agent looked at the address Loretta had written on a small piece of paper. "It's close by, ma'am. Take Railroad Street as you exit the station, and then turn onto Pryor Street. The restaurant is on Pryor."

Loretta walked at a brisk pace, as though an unseen hand pulled her forward. She practically quivered for want of food and rest. The day was warm and humid, with a blue, cloudless sky overhead. Lovely Southern belles, reduced to genteel poverty after the War between the States, strolled the sidewalks in their out-of-fashion attire. A group of young boys crouched over a game of marbles, while the bustle of rebuilding echoed all around her.

Loretta glanced at the address on the paper in her hand and then at the addresses on the buildings. According to the numbers, she was nearing Cousin Lil's address.

Finally, she reached the building that matched the address on her slip of paper. But her heart sank. On the large wooden door a sign read *CLOSED. MOVED TO MISSISSIPPI.*

Loretta gasped as despair entwined itself around her soul, strangling all hope. This could not be. Why would Cousin Lil have moved? And why would she have moved without notifying Loretta? It was unlike Lil to do so.

Her head spinning with questions and even more so with fear, Loretta sat down on the stoop and buried her head in her hands. With no money left, she could not return to Cape May. Nor could she remain in Atlanta.

What should she do? Where should she turn?

Ebony's voice rose from the depth of her spirit: *Turn to God. He will never fail you.*

If ever Loretta was in an impossible situation, it

was now. If ever she needed the God of the Impossible, it was now.

God, show me what to do? Help me!

But all she heard was silence.

Saturday, June 21, 1873

After being discharged from the hospital, Jeremiah settled into his room at the boardinghouse. He worried that Loretta had not come to visit him in two days. It was unlike her, especially since she'd been so solicitous about his health. Had something happened to her? Had Tom Brogan taken advantage of Jeremiah's absence to harass her? Or—banish the thought—to harm her?

Jeremiah struggled to calm his fear. He chose to think the best. He'd send a message to Clarissa to determine if Loretta was all right. Loretta had told him she'd be staying with the Steubens, at least until she found another job.

He searched for paper and pen in the desk drawer. He'd write a note and ask the landlord of the boardinghouse to have someone deliver it to Clarissa's home.

Jeremiah took a deep breath.

My Dearest Loretta,

I have been discharged from the hospital and am currently staying at the Cape May Boardinghouse under strict orders from my doctor to get as much rest as possible.

I am concerned that I have not heard from you. Are you all right? Ever since that episode in the store with Tom Brogan, I have no rest when you are not with me.

I trust, nonetheless, that you are well. I assume that you are still staying with Clarissa and John. Please let me know.

Sincerely,

Jeremiah Collins

He re-read the letter. There was something missing. He added a postscript.

P. S. I miss you.

. . .

Satisfied, he sealed the letter and then took it to the landlord's office. A young man sat at a desk in front of a ledger book.

"Excuse me. Is there someone who could deliver this letter for me to an address on the other side of town?"

The young man rose and smiled. "By all means, sir. I will deliver it myself. It's one of my duties as clerk."

"Thank you." Jeremiah offered him payment, but the young man refused.

"It is my pleasure to serve you, sir." With that, he took the letter from Jeremiah's hand. "I will deliver it right away." He pointed to the ledger on his desk. "I was just thinking that I needed a break from the boredom of financial calculations." He chuckled.

"I understand. I had similar feelings when I had my business."

"Oh? What kind of business did you own?"

Jeremiah grew solemn. "I owned the fishing supply store here in town. The one that burned down a few days ago."

Compassion flooded the young man's face. "Oh, my. Yes, I heard about the fire. I am so sorry. Has the arsonist been found yet?"

Jeremiah raised an eyebrow. "So you know that arson is suspected?"

"Yes. It's been all over the news."

"I see. I've been in the hospital being treated for smoke inhalation. I must get myself a newspaper to catch up."

The young man reached into the top drawer of his desk. "Here. Please. Take mine. It's this morning's edition."

Jeremiah took the newspaper and thanked the clerk.

"Now, I will get your letter delivered right away, sir." The clerk left, and Jeremiah returned to his room.

Once inside, he sat down at the kitchen table and opened the newspaper. A headline jumped out at him: *Suspected arson under investigation in fishing supply store fire*. The article stated that the police were on the lookout for any clues as to the origin of the fire. Residents were urged to report anything that looked suspicious, no matter how minor.

Jeremiah released a long sigh. Loretta suspected Tom Brogan. What if she were right? The very thought of it stung Jeremiah to the core. Being betrayed by a stranger was one thing, but being betrayed by a friend was quite another.

Like Jesus being betrayed by Judas.

The emotional agony of what the Lord must have suffered struck Jeremiah with unprecedented force.

He folded the newspaper, rested his elbows on the table, and prayed. He needed to get in touch with Loretta as soon as possible. She'd become like the air he needed to breathe.

About an hour later, the clerk appeared at Jeremiah's door, the letter still in his hand. "Mr. Collins, I'm sorry to say that Mrs. Vye has left town."

Jeremiah's soul shook. "Left town? But how can that be?"

"Mrs. Steubens told me that Mrs. Vye left last evening for Atlanta, Georgia, in search of work. Mrs. Steubens planned to pay you a visit upon your discharge from the hospital to notify you herself."

Jeremiah sank into the nearest chair. Why had Loretta not told him she'd decided to leave for Atlanta? Why had she left so suddenly? Worst of all, why had she not bid him farewell?

His heart broken, he thanked the clerk. Perhaps he'd been right in not proclaiming his love for Loretta. In not proposing marriage. If she loved him, she wouldn't have left without even so much as a goodbye.

Chapter Sixteen

Saturday, June 21, 1873

Loretta didn't know how long she'd remained on the stoop of what used to be Cousin Lil's restaurant. All she knew was that when she awakened, it was dusk.

And a policeman stood over her.

"Are you all right, miss?"

She immediately rose. "Yes. Yes. I'm so sorry. I must have fallen asleep."

The officer placed his hands on his hips. "Well, this ain't no place for a woman to fall asleep, miss. If I was you, I'd get myself on home as fast as I could." His tone was firm yet fatherly.

She struggled to clear the fog from her head. "Yes. You're right." She looked to the right and to the left.

The officer's eyes studied her. "You got a home, ain't you?"

"Yes, sir."

"Where is it? I'll make sure you get there safely."

She rubbed her forehead. "Uh, I mean no. No, sir." What could she say? "Well, you see, Officer, my home is in Cape May, New Jersey. But it burned down, so I came down here to stay with my cousin, who used to own a restaurant at this address. But when I got here, I saw the sign on the door that says she's moved to Mississippi."

The officer looked at her askance and then walked up to the door to read the sign. He turned to Loretta. "You talkin' about Lil's Restaurant?"

"Yes, sir. Lil is my cousin."

"Fine cook, that Lil. And even a finer woman. Too bad she had to leave town. Not enough business here to support her."

Loretta let out a sigh of relief. "So you know Lil?"

He nodded. "Used to bring my wife here to eat pretty much every week. Best collard greens in town, I tell you."

"I'm glad to hear that." Loretta smiled. "So then, Officer, perhaps you can help me. Now that I've discovered Cousin Lil is no longer here, I have no place to stay. Is there a church nearby that could take me in for a night? In the morning, I'll need to find a way to head home to New Jersey."

The officer rubbed his salt-and-pepper beard and then looked up with a smile. "Yes'm, there is. Old Pastor Perry's church be but a block away from here. His wife, Miz Abigail, be one of the kindest ladies in all Atlanta. Let me take you there."

"That would be perfect. Thank you so very much." Loretta rose, smoothed the front of her skirt and followed the police officer. Her heart ached for Jeremiah. For the ladies of her knitting circle. For Cape May. What a fool she'd been to leave them!

In a few moments, they reached an old church, next to which stood a humble parsonage. The church's white, stucco exterior had turned a shade of dingy gray. A few cracked panels of the stained glass windows seemed about ready to fall out. But the Cross on the very top shone like gold in the soft, evening twilight.

Next to the church, the parsonage stood as a fitting companion. Just as old and dilapidated, it held, nonetheless, a homespun charm that invited the lost and the weary.

The officer knocked on the door.

A gray-haired, middle-aged woman answered with

a smile. "Why, if it ain't Officer Jones. What you doin' here this time o' day? Ain't seen you at church for a while now."

The officer hung his head and shuffled. "Been workin' on Sundays, Miz Abigail." He quickly changed the subject and turned toward Loretta. "I got somebody here in need of y'all's help."

Miz Abigail gave Loretta a smile that heightened the warm tones of her chocolate skin. "What can I do for you, chile?"

Loretta explained her situation.

"Why, then, you come right on in. We keep a guest room for the likes of you." She placed a hand on Loretta's shoulder. "Not meanin' no disrespect. Just that all people is welcome in Abigail Perry's home."

The officer settled his hat back on his head. "Thank ye, Miz Abigail. I best be gettin' back to my beat."

"You're welcome." As the police officer left, Miz Abigail waved him off. "Don't you be missin' no more church on Sundays, you hear me, Officer Jones?"

But he was already out of earshot.

Abigail put an arm around Loretta's shoulders. "Come on in. I gonna fix you some of my famous beef stew and then we can talk."

A few moments later, Miz Abigail brought out

two steaming bowls of her rich beef stew and placed them on the table. The aroma reminded Loretta of how hungry she was. She'd eaten only an apple cake all day.

Miz Abigail said the blessing. "Now then, tell me what brings you here to Atlanta."

"I'm badly in need of a job. My husband died in a shipwreck in April, leaving me a destitute widow. I had a job in Cape May, New Jersey, but a fire destroyed the building and my apartment and left me without work. I came to Atlanta to work in my cousin's restaurant, but when I got to her place, I found a sign on the door that said she'd moved to Mississippi." Loretta paused. "So, now, here I am. Trying to figure out a way to get back to New Jersey. I spent my last dime on a one-way ticket."

Miz Abigail put a hand on Loretta's arm. "That must have been right hard for you. Losin' your husband and all."

Hot tears stung Loretta's eyes. "Yes, it was very difficult. The worst of it was that he went bankrupt shortly before he died, leaving me with no financial support."

Miz Abigail thought a moment. "So you be needin' a job, you say?"

"Yes."

The old woman looked at Loretta for a long moment. “Would you be willin' to stay here in Atlanta?”

Loretta gave her a questioning look.

“The church here be lookin' for a secretary. Our last one done up and left all of the sudden last week. Said she needed to be movin' on to better pastures. “ Miz Abigail sighed and shook her head. “I don't know what better pastures there be than a church, but, to each his own.” She looked pointedly at Loretta. “So ... would you be interested in takin' over her job? I can’t promise it’ll be easy, what with all the segregation still goin’ on after the War between the States.”

Loretta pondered her options. If she stayed in Atlanta, she might never see Jeremiah again. But if she didn't stay, she'd be homeless. Hadn't she left him already to work at Cousin Lil's restaurant?

“Yes. Yes I would be very interested. But, I don't have any money to rent a place to live.”

Miz Abigail smiled. “Don't you worry. A place to live comes with the job. It's nothing more than a room, but it'll do until you save enough to rent a bigger place.”

Loretta's heart leapt. For the first time since the fire, confidence rose within her. “I'll take the job.”

Miz Abigail slapped a hand on the table and

shouted."Praise the Lord! You can start Monday mornin'. The pay will be seven dollars a week plus meals here in my kitchen." Miz Abigail laughed. "I be the cook for the parsonage as well as bein' the pastor's wife."

Loretta's soul linked to this woman. They would be good friends, she was sure. "I'm so thankful for your help."

Miz Abigail shook her head. "Don't thank me." She pointed heavenward. "Thank the good Lord above. He takes care of His chil'en and meets our every need." She rose.

"And now, you best be gettin' some rest. Church starts at nine o'clock tomorrow mornin', and we can't be late. Ole Pastor Perry don't like it when I's late. Says it gives a bad example." She chuckled. "And he's right."

Sunday, June 22, 1873

The church service the next morning was unlike anything Loretta had ever attended. First of all, she was the only white woman present among a sea of curious faces in all shades of brown. All eyes were glued to her as she walked down the aisle to the front pew with Miz Abigail. For one who hated to be in the limelight, the experience was an ordeal of the first order.

Heat rose to Loretta's face. What did these people think of her? Would they accept her? Or would they reject her because of the color of her skin?

The organist intoned the first hymn, *I'm Gonna Sing Till the Spirit Moves.* The congregation stood and, in short order, began clapping their hands to the joyful tune. Before it was over, people were literally dancing for joy up and down the aisle.

Despite Miz Abigail's prodding, Loretta remained in her seat. Yet, there was something about the guileless spontaneity of the people that deeply moved her. They truly loved and believed this Lord about whom they were singing. Had their suffering made them more sensitive to Him?

Would her suffering make her more sensitive to Him? Was that the ultimate purpose of suffering? To turn one's attention toward God?

After the service, Miz Abigail introduced Loretta to some members of the congregation. Each warmly welcomed her as though she were one of their own.

If this were any indication of her new home, Loretta was going to like it here.

* * *

Sunday, June 22, 1873

That afternoon, after a hearty lunch with Miz Abigail, Pastor Perry, and Elder Canton Munroe and his wife, Gladys, Loretta retreated to her room. She needed to write a letter to Jeremiah, explaining why she'd left so suddenly and to make him aware of the gossip about her and Tom Brogan that was fast spreading around Cape May.

The lying words she'd heard in the general store still stung. And stung deeply. How could she ever face Jeremiah and her church family in Cape May again? How could she ever face the women in her knitting circle? Would they believe the cruel allegation? Or would they defend her innocence?

Most of all, what about Jeremiah? Would he trust his friend more than he trusted her? After all, he'd known Tom for three years. He known her for only two months.

Even if they all believed she was completely innocent, they would never look at her the same way again. A tainted reputation could never be totally cleared. Gossip had a way of doing that to its victim.

And she was that victim.

She took a sheet of paper from the desk drawer in the guest room. She laid it on the desk and reached for the quill pen and ink.

My Dear Jeremiah,

I trust that you are much improved after your terrible ordeal. By now you may have learned that I am in Atlanta. I came in response to my cousin's earlier invitation to work in her restaurant. Unfortunately, when I arrived, there was a sign on her restaurant door stating that she had moved to Mississippi.

Through a series of providential circumstances, the good Lord led me to the home of a pastor and his wife who offered me a position as the church secretary. I considered this offer a miracle from the Lord and accepted the position on the spot.

I am well and hope the same of you, although I must say that I miss you very much. You have likely been distressed over my sudden departure. Shortly before I left, I overheard two women gossiping about me in the general store. Their comments made my face burn with shame. Of course, they were all lies. But I was afraid that once those lies spread throughout Cape May, because of your association with me, your reputation would be irrevocably injured. I determined to spare you that shame by leaving immediately. I am hoping that being out of sight will keep me out of the minds of those whose only pleasure is to vilify me.

I do hope that you can come for a visit in the near future. If not, I invite you to write. I would more than welcome your missives.

More than anything, I would like to return to my beloved Cape May one day. But whether I do or not is in the Lord's hands.

In case you wish to write to me, I am currently staying in a room kindly provided as part of my salary by Pastor and Mrs. Abigail Perry of Amazing Grace Church in Atlanta. My address is 1215 Pryor Street, in care of the Perry Family.

Please give Burrows a hug for me.

Your faithful and devoted friend,
Loretta Vye

She held the letter in her hand and re-read it. Had she given Jeremiah sufficient indication of her feelings for him? While she didn't want to be too forward, she did want him to understand that leaving him had broken her heart.

Satisfied with what she'd written, she proceeded to seal the envelope but stopped. With tears welling up in her eyes, she kissed the envelope and prayed that Jeremiah would reciprocate her feelings.

Then, sealing the letter, she left it on the desk, to go out with the morning mail.

Chapter Seventeen

Monday, June 23, 1873

While the boardinghouse provided a good temporary shelter for Jeremiah, he was eager to leave it behind to resume his normal life. He needed to get his business up and running again as soon as possible. Otherwise, his customers would get their supplies elsewhere.

Not that there were many fishing supply stores in the area. But it wouldn't be too difficult for them to go to other towns to purchase supplies.

But he could do nothing until he heard from his insurance company. Although he'd put away a decent sum for a rainy day, it was not enough to purchase a new building. And that was what he needed first. A new building in which to resume his business. Unless, of course, his insurance money proved sufficient to rebuild on the site of the old one. That would make things a whole lot easier.

But since when was life easy?

The fire had forced him to reconsider his life. His priorities. And Loretta. He found himself thinking of her incessantly. He'd been on the brink of proposing marriage when the fire shattered his plans. Now she was gone. And she'd taken his heart with her.

He stared out the window. *This, too, shall pass.* His mother often spoke those words in times of difficulty. He could still hear the hope in her voice as she uttered them. It was good to remember that earthly suffering was temporary. What mattered most was to avoid eternal suffering by believing in Jesus Christ. Eternity was forever.

He drew out his pocket watch. Today was the day he'd arranged to meet with the insurance adjustor to survey the site of the fire prior to filing an insurance claim. The weather was overcast, portending a storm. He prayed that the rain would hold off until afterward.

As Jeremiah approached the scorched building, his heart sank in his chest. Only the frame remained. Everything inside had been destroyed. All his supplies. All his furnishings. Everything. Shards of blackened debris littered the entire interior of the building. His little back apartment was now only a hole. The roof, a flat pile of rubble. Thank God that his and Loretta's lives had been spared.

But why?

His lower lip quivered as he blinked back stinging tears. Years of hard work and struggle had ended in defeat. It was enough to shake a man to his very core.

If only the passerby had gotten a clearer description of the person trespassing on the night of the fire.

"Mr. Collins, I presume?" Jeremiah turned toward the voice behind him.

The insurance adjustor approached him. "Good morning. I'm Elliott Wilson."

Jeremiah offered a tentative smile and extended a hand. "Pleased to meet you, Mr. Wilson."

The adjustor returned the handshake. "Well, I won't keep you long. Do you mind if I take a look around?"

"Please. Feel free to do your job as you see fit."

Mr. Wilson asked Jeremiah a few preliminary questions, after which he searched the backyard while Jeremiah waited.

Finally, Mr. Wilson returned to Jeremiah. "Based on the eyewitness report of the passerby and on my preliminary investigation, I have a feeling that the fire started in the rear of the building. Come. I'll show you."

Jeremiah followed him there. The fire had made the backyard treacherous to walk upon in parts. Holes had appeared in some places.

As Mr. Wilson surveyed the property, he stopped suddenly and stared at something on the ground.

Jeremiah followed his gaze, noting the small object lying half hidden in the soil.

The adjustor stooped down to pick it up and studied it for a moment, turning it over and over in his hand. He then faced Jeremiah. "Have you ever seen this before?"

Jeremiah instantly recognized Tom Brogan's penknife. "May I take a closer look?"

The adjustor nodded and handed the knife to Jeremiah.

Sure enough, the initials *T.B.* were carved on the handle. There was no doubt. It was Tom's knife.

A pang of deep sorrow flooded Jeremiah's soul. "This belongs to my friend Tom Brogan. He showed it to me shortly after he purchased it. I recognize it by his carved initials."

Mr. Wilson let out a low whistle. "Well, if this indicates what I think it does, Tom Brogan is not your friend."

Jeremiah swallowed hard as the sting of betrayal pierced his heart. But there had to be a mistake. Maybe someone had gotten a hold of Tom's penknife to blackmail him. Tom simply could not be the culprit. "Tom can be an ornery guy, but I find it impossible to believe that he would burn down my store. Is there a way to check for fingerprints?"

"You would have to call the police." The adjustor sighed. "Something I would definitely suggest you do. It will support your insurance claim."

"I'll report the incident to the police on my way back to the boardinghouse." He placed the penknife securely in his pocket. "Thanks for your help."

"Sure thing." Mr. Wilson made a note of his finding. "I'm going to finish walking around the premises to make some notes and then head back to my office. It will take a few days for the insurance company to review your claim. Once done, I will send you the report."

"I hope it's a good one."

"I hope so too." Mr. Wilson smiled. "The discovery of that penknife gives you a good foundation to stand on for full compensation."

"That's a blessing. Thank you. Do you need me here any longer?

"No, sir."

Jeremiah left and headed toward the police station on his way back to the boardinghouse. Dark clouds overhead threatened a downpour. He hoped it wouldn't start raining before he got home. Or at least to his temporary home. He missed his store and his tiny apartment in the back.

He missed Loretta even more. Would he ever see her again?

Was she lost to him forever in Atlanta?

As he reached the police station, he whispered a prayer for favor with the insurance company. If he could recoup the full value of the building, he could start over again.

Maybe he could even convince Loretta to be his wife.

Monday, June 23, 1873

The next morning, Loretta took her letter to Jeremiah to the post office. She prayed he would receive it with a heart of forgiveness for her sudden departure and compassion for the insult to her character.

She breathed in the fresh air of downtown Atlanta

as she walked back to the church. The day was bright and sunny. The city bustled with life and friendliness. Wherever she turned, people smiled and bid her good day. Hope rose within her.

Today was her first day on the job as church secretary. Miz Abigail would meet her at nine o'clock to explain her duties.

Upon arriving at the church, Loretta found Miz Abigail in the secretary's office reprimanding a boy of about seven years. "Now you know better than to steal, young man, and especially to steal from a church. Why would you do such a despicable thing?"

"I was hungry, Miz Abigail. I ain't had nothin' to eat since the day before yesterday."

Loretta's heart went out to the boy.

Miz Abigail patted the his head. "Well, then, all you need to do is ask me for somethin' to eat, and I'll surely give it to you." She placed a hand on his shoulder. "Now, you repent before the Lord, and He'll forgive you."

The boy lowered his head. "I'm sorry for stealin', Lord Jesus. Please forgive me."

Miz Abigail smiled. "Now, that's good. That's real good."

The boy looked up at her. "Would you give me somethin' to eat now, Miz Abigail?"

She smiled at him. “Come with me.” She informed Loretta that she'd be back in a moment.

While Miz Abigail tended to the child, Loretta looked around her new office. It was small but orderly. A tall, narrow window in front of the desk overlooked a lovely little backyard filled with blossoming daisies. In one corner of the office stood a lush philodendron plant. To the left side of the desk stood a bookcase filled with Bibles and other Christian reading material. On the wall hung an old wooden Cross.

Miz Abigail returned. “I don't know what to do with that boy. He be Miz Olson's youngest. Always gettin' into trouble for stealin'. Always say it's 'cause he's hungry.”

Something stirred in Loretta’s soul. “Does your church have a children's ministry?”

“Used to. But the woman who ran it got married and moved to Oklahoma. So we's been without one for a while now.”

“Would you mind if I worked with the children?”

Miz Abigail's eyes widened. “That would be wonderful.”

“I love children. My late husband Edward and I were unable to have children.”

“Then you be the right person. The Bible done say

that the good Lord makes the barren woman the mother of many children."

Loretta swallowed hard. Did the Lord love her enough to do that for her?

Miz Abigail chuckled. "Well, now. First things first. Let me explain your duties as the church secretary, and then I'll explain your duties as our new head of children's ministry."

Trying not to be overwhelmed, Loretta took in Miz Abigail's instructions. By the time the dear lady had finished, Loretta had a feeling that she was in Atlanta to stay.

Monday, June 23, 1873

Back at the boardinghouse, Jeremiah settled into a chair with both his Bible and Burrows on his lap. A knock at the door almost immediately caused him to rise again.

He got up and opened the door to find Tom Brogan in the hallway. Jeremiah's chest constricted. "Hello, Tom."

"Mind if I come in?"

Jeremiah hesitated and then opened the door.

Holding his hat in his hands, Tom staggered into the room, leaving the door open behind him. "I ain't plannin' to stay. Just wanted to tell you somethin' you may be needin' to know."

Jeremiah's spirit went on high alert. Was Tom about to confess? "You've been drinkin' again, Tom. What do you have to tell me?"

Tom fumbled his hat. "That woman you had workin' in your store." He slurred his words. "She lied to you."

Every muscle in Jeremiah's body tensed. "What do you mean, she lied?"

"I mean I did her no harm the day I was in your store. 'Twas the other way around." He coughed and averted his eyes. "She tried to seduce me."

Fire rose in Jeremiah's belly. "How dare you say such a thing about Loretta? Why, she's the godliest woman I know."

Tom snorted. "Don't be so sure. Things ain't always what they seem."

Jeremiah studied Tom's shifting eyes. "If you dare speak such a despicable thing about her again, I will have you reported to the police for slander."

He snarled. "Before you get so high 'n' mighty in your britches, Jeremiah, ask yourself this question.

Why did she leave town so fast if she wasn't guilty? Did she even say goodbye to you?"

Jeremiah narrowed his eyes. "How did you know she left?"

Tom lifted his chin. "I got my connections."

Jeremiah remained silent.

Tom smirked, turned to leave, and then looked back. "Oh, and one more thing. She started the fire, not me."

Tom had just walked into his own trap by defending himself.

"Who was accusing you, Tom?"

"Just wanted you to know for sure that I didn't start the fire."

"Well, I got proof you did."

Tom's face paled. "What kind o' proof?"

Jeremiah withdrew the penknife from his pocket. "This kind." He paused. "Yeah, Tom. You're right. Things aren't always what they seem. It seemed as though you were my friend."

Tom lunged for the knife, but Jeremiah pushed him to the floor before he could grab it. Jeremiah placed a foot on Tom's chest, but, drunk as he was, there was no risk that he would get up.

"Is everything all right, Mr. Collins?" The landlord

stood at the open door. "I heard a lot of commotion and wanted to check on you."

"I'm all right. Please call the police right away and tell them we've found our arsonist."

"Yes, sir."

In a few moments, the police arrived at Jeremiah's room, clasped handcuffs on Tom Brogan, and took him to jail.

Jeremiah sat down with a sigh. "Lord, forgive him, for he doesn't know what he's doing."

Chapter Eighteen

Tuesday, June 24, 1873

Loretta's first day as church secretary proved very rewarding. If only the church were located in Cape May. Jeremiah was never far from her mind. She missed him greatly. Did he miss her as well?

Perhaps if she worked hard and saved her money, she could one day return to Cape May and open that knitting shop her knitting circle friends had suggested. She filed the dream away in her heart.

At the sound of rustling on her second morning at work, Loretta looked up. There at her office door stood the Olson boy. "Why, hello!" Loretta gave him a warm smile.

"You be our new church secretary?" The boy's eyes were wide.

"Yes. My name is Mrs. Vye."

He remained in the doorway. "Pleased to meet you, Mrs. Vye."

"I'm pleased to meet you too. What is your name?"

"Booker Olson, and I be seven years old."

"Seven? Why, you're almost a man!"

Booker's face broke into a broad grin.

Loretta tilted her head. "Do you know what *Booker* means?"

He shook his head. "No, ma'am."

"It means *scribe*."

"What *scribe* mean?"

"A scribe is someone who keeps records of things or who writes."

"Like what you do?"

Loretta laughed. "Yes, like what I do."

"But I don't know how to write."

Loretta's heart dropped. "Would you like me to teach you?"

He nodded. "But, first, I best be askin' my mama."

"Yes, of course. Ask your mama first. That's the right thing to do."

"Okay, bye." In a flash, he disappeared.

Loretta leaned against the back of her chair and

smiled. She had a strong sensation that God was doing a deep work in her life. What it was, she wasn't sure. But one thing she did know for sure. It had everything to do with restoring her soul.

Tuesday, June 24, 1873

Tom Brogan's visit had left Jeremiah in an emotional shambles. His blood boiled at the accusation about Loretta. What scum of a man would make such an accusation, and for what reason? It was one thing to destroy a person's property, but it was quite another to destroy a person's reputation. And Loretta wasn't even here to defend herself.

Yes, Tom was jealous of Jeremiah. But, why? So far, there was nothing official between him and Loretta. In fact, there was nothing even unofficial between them. Jeremiah had never expressed his love for her–a fact he now deeply regretted—nor she for him. So, what roused Tom's vicious comments other than the fact she'd had no time for him? That she despised him?

Why then, had Loretta left so abruptly, without

even saying goodbye? Had she been afraid to face him? Or was it a way of hiding guilt?

The tormenting thoughts bombarded Jeremiah's mind like relentless bullets, threatening to destroy his sanity. Jeremiah raked his fingers through his hair. He had to talk with Loretta, but how? When? She was eight hundred miles away. And he was not yet well enough to travel.

He rubbed his forehead. He had a choice to make. Would he believe Tom Brogan, or would he believe Loretta Vye?

He took a deep breath. In the depths of his soul, his choice was already made.

Tuesday, June 24, 1873

Later that afternoon, Jeremiah received a visit from John and Clarissa Steubens.

After taking a seat with her husband John on the settee across from Jeremiah, Clarissa folded her hands in her lap. "I promised Loretta I would notify you that she's left for Atlanta. Your landlord, of course, preempted my visit, but I felt obliged to come myself as I had promised her."

John grunted in agreement.

Jeremiah sat forward, his gaze fixed on Clarissa. "Yes, thank you for coming. I can't deny that I was deeply surprised and hurt that Loretta left without saying goodbye."

Clarissa shifted in her chair. "Yes. I understand. It is so unlike her. Something must have happened for her to act in such a manner. I could tell she left in a state of intense turmoil."

Jeremiah grew pensive. "I think I may know the reason."

Clarissa gave him a questioning look.

"Apparently, there are vicious rumors spreading of some improprieties on Loretta's part."

Clarissa's eyes widened. "Improprieties? Impossible! What sort of improprieties? And who would imply such a horrendous thing?"

Jeremiah hesitated. "Tom Brogan stopped by this morning. He accused Loretta of seducing him the day she was alone minding the store."

Clarissa's face turned red. "Surely, you don't believe him?"

"Absolutely not. I was furious that he'd had the

gall to make such horrific accusations, and I expressed my fury in no uncertain terms."

Clarissa sighed. "Poor, dear Loretta. She bore this all alone." Tears glistened in her eyes. "But why did she not tell us?"

Jeremiah shook his head. "I don't know. Perhaps she did not want to cause us further pain." He lowered his head. "In any case, she's gone now." An ache lodged in his throat.

Clarissa rose and paced the room. "We must find her. We must tell her that we don't believe a word of these vicious accusations and that we will defend her reputation to the end." She wrung her hands. "But I don't know how to get in touch with her. I don't even know her cousin's name. All I know is that she owns a restaurant in Atlanta."

John intervened. "Well, that's a starting point. Perhaps we could telegraph the police department in Atlanta for help."

"What about Tom Brogan? What will happen to him now that he's been arrested?"

Jeremiah sighed. "He'll go to trial of course, but the evidence against him is overwhelming."

Clarissa leaned forward. "What do you think motivated Tom to burn down your store and to slander Loretta?"

Jeremiah thought a moment. "I suppose that, deep down, he really wanted her for himself and was angry that she didn't want him. When he first mentioned his interest in Loretta, I thought he was only joking. Then, when he noticed that she was interested in me, I think something triggered inside him."

John nodded. "The true colors of a man come out under pressure."

Jeremiah knit his brows. "I guess I didn't know Tom as well as I thought. Makes me feel bad I didn't notice it sooner. Maybe I could have helped him."

"Maybe so," John offered. "But, bottomline, a man makes his own choices."

Jeremiah rubbed the back of his neck. "Yep. Bottomline, he does."

Chapter Nineteen

Thursday, July 3, 1873

To his great relief, several days later Jeremiah received a letter from Loretta. In it she told him that upon arriving in Atlanta, she'd discovered that her cousin had moved to Mississippi. Through a series of providential circumstances, Loretta had found a job and a place to live through the help of the kind pastor's wife at Amazing Grace Church, now her address and her new church home.

Jeremiah eagerly read every word, thanking God again and again that Loretta was safe. She even sounded happy.

His heart lurched. What if she decided to remain

in Atlanta forever? What if she met a fine man there? What if she forgot Jeremiah altogether?

He swallowed hard. Although he greatly missed her, he desired nothing more than her happiness.

O God, he prayed, *watch over Loretta. You know I love her, Lord. But I yield my will to Yours. Just make clear to me what Your will is. And if it is that I not marry Loretta, then quiet this tormenting ache in my soul.*

Monday, July 7, 1873

Two weeks after meeting with the insurance adjustor, Jeremiah received a letter from him. The claim had been approved for full reimbursement of damages. Jeremiah was now free to rebuild his building, his business, and his life.

Tears stung his eyes. "Thank You, Lord! Thank You for restoring what the locust had eaten."

His hope renewed, Jeremiah began plans to rebuild on the same spot. If all went well, within the year he would reopen his store. Meanwhile, there was a lot to do, not the least of which was to make sure that Loretta Vye knew she still had a job if she wanted it.

He went to his desk and withdrew a sheet of paper from the top drawer. He dipped his quill pen into the inkwell on top of the desk and began to write.

My dearest Loretta,

It is with great joy that I write to inform you that I shall soon begin rebuilding my store on the same lot. The insurance company approved my claim, especially since we had tangible proof of arson with the discovery of Tom Brogan's penknife in the backyard.

I want you to know that if you are still interested, your job awaits you.

Your faithful and devoted,
Jeremiah

Loretta's heart soared upon receiving Jeremiah's letter. His offer to restore her job moved her deeply, but she was not quite yet ready to accept it. Being in Atlanta had proven a balm to her broken soul. Through Miz

Abigail's wise counsel, she was learning about and embracing her true identity in Christ. The Lord was making her whole. He was teaching her to depend only on Him.

Being far from Cape May had also given Loretta a new perspective on her life. She'd begun to discern the manner in which her choices had stifled her growth. The manner in which she'd trusted more in man than in God. The manner in which she'd allowed Satan to derail her from her destiny through his lies.

Molly had been right. Men and women were equal in value, although different in function. Submitting to God-ordained authority did not mean submerging one's personal identity in the identity of another. It did not mean allowing oneself to be controlled by another through the power of provision or persuasion.

On the contrary, submission to God-ordained authority meant serving with love and humility the one whom God had placed in authority, as though one were serving the Lord Himself. The only one in whom she needed to submerge herself was Jesus Christ.

Why had it taken her so long to learn these truths? Why had it taken her so long to embrace her dignity as a daughter of the King of kings?

Yet the important thing was that she *was* learning these truths. She was embracing them and allowing herself to be transformed by them. She was experiencing the freedom that came only with applying them to her life.

You shall know the truth, and the truth shall make you free. One of Mama's favorite Scripture verses. It now meant so much more to her. The lie enslaved; the truth set free. The greatest slavery was internal. Slavery of the soul.

Yes. Only the truth could set one free.

And Truth was Christ Himself.

Miz Abigail had already discovered this. And now, the dear woman had been helping Loretta discover it as well. As the Word commanded in Romans 12:2, Loretta was learning how to change her thinking to align with God's thinking and in so doing, she was discovering His perfect will for her life.

Maybe one day, she'd be ready to return to Cape May—and to Jeremiah. But before then, the Lord still had some internal healing to do in her soul.

Chapter Twenty

A year later . . .

Monday, June 8, 1874

With great thanksgiving in his heart, Jeremiah stood in front of his brand-new fishing supplies store. The bright afternoon sun splashed joy all over the new brick structure. His heart soared. It was even finer than the original store. He'd extended the length and added a second large room in the hope that Loretta would return and open a knitting shop there.

As the weeks and months had passed by, Jeremiah's heart longed more and more for her. Her absence had only deepened his love to the point that he could not imagine his life without her. Day after day, he prayed that the Lord would move on her heart to return to Cape May. And to him.

Over the last several months, he'd kept in close correspondence with Loretta, and she, with him. She seemed happy in Georgia. He didn't want to disrupt that happiness. Yet she'd frequently tell him she missed him. But did she miss him enough to return to Cape May?

Often, he'd considered joining her in Atlanta. But the nature of his business and his well-established clientèle required that he remain near the coast. He knew no other trade.

His stomach roiling, he sighed and shoved his hands in his pockets. What if Loretta did not love him the way he loved her? What if she had no intention of ever returning to Cape May?

What if she fell in love with someone else?

He chided himself for his failure to act. That would end today. He would be more forthright in his declaration of love for her. He would write and tell her all that lay on his heart. He would ask her to marry him and let the chips fall where they may.

But, in his heart of hearts, he prayed they'd fall in his favor.

* * *

Monday, June 8, 1874

A year had already transpired since Loretta first began her job at Amazing Grace Church. While she'd loved serving in her capacity as church secretary and children's ministry leader, lately she'd become restless and extremely homesick for Cape May.

"Chile," Miz Abigail patted Loretta's hand as they drank coffee in Miz Abigail's kitchen. "Sometimes restlessness be a sign that Holy Spirit be wantin' to move you to a new field of ministry." Miz Abigail took a sip of her steaming brew.

"But how can I know for sure? I have a good life here. A job I love and a wonderful church family. Why do I even feel this way?"

"Well, what you be thinkin' 'bout most?"

Heat rose to Loretta's face. She gave a sheepish smile. "Truth be told, I think constantly of Jeremiah."

Miz Abigail grinned. "You love him, don't you?"

Loretta gulped and then nodded. "I've never loved a man in the way I love him. Being away from him for a year has only deepened my love for him."

"And how he be feelin' 'bout you?"

"He loves me too. He's told me so in his letters—well, in so many words."

"Has he made you an offer of marriage?"

"Not yet. But I think he's afraid because he doesn't want to rob me of my happiness here in Georgia with y'all."

Miz Abigail laughed a hearty laugh. "I see you've become a Southerner." She emphasized *y'all.*

Loretta giggled in reply.

Miz Abigail grew serious. "Lemme ask you this. What is your treasure?"

Loretta furrowed her brows. "What do you mean, Miz Abigail?"

"I mean what do you treasure most on earth?"

"Why, my relationship with the Lord."

"Yes. Yes, of course. But I mean, is there someone or somethin' on this earth—here and now—that you treasure most?"

Loretta didn't have to think about her answer. "Jeremiah."

"Then that's where your heart is. The Good Book done say that 'where your treasure is, there your heart will be also.'"

Suddenly, the answer was clear. "I need to go back to Cape May and marry Jeremiah."

Miz Abigail nodded. "I think so, too, chile. I think that be the path the good Lord has for you."

Tears welled up in Loretta's eyes. Tears of joy at

God's faithfulness. And tears of sorrow at having to leave Miz Abigail and the brothers and sisters of Amazing Grace Church.

Loretta placed a hand on Miz Abigail's. "I'll be forever indebted to you, Miz Abigail. When I came here a year ago, I was a confused, frightened, and hurting woman who barely trusted God. Nor did I trust in the abilities He'd given me. But now I'm no longer afraid. He's shown me that I'm competent and capable because of His grace. That I can do all things through Christ who gives me strength."

"Well, you sure done did an amazin' job as our church secretary." Miz Abigail emphasized the word *amazing* and laughed. "Did you get it? *Amazin'* Grace Church?"

Loretta gave her a heartfelt smile.

Tears glistened in Miz Abigail's eyes. "We gonna miss you, Miz Loretta. Miss you bad." Miz Abigail leaned toward Loretta and patted her hand. "But you doin' the right thing, chile. You doin' the right thing."

In the depths of her heart, Loretta agreed. She was doing the right thing by going home to Cape May to marry Jeremiah. She was whole. She didn't *need* Jeremiah Collins. She *wanted* him. And that made her ready to marry him, to move into the next phase of growth—the stage of interdependence.

And she'd rather not be interdependent with anyone else in the whole world than Jeremiah Collins.

Yes, she was ready to marry the captain. But was he ready to marry her?

Booker Olson ran into Loretta's office where she was seated at her desk. “Mrs. Vye! Mrs. Vye! The postman done asked me to give you this letter. Said I was a big boy now, and he could trust me.” A broad grin spread across the boy's face.

Loretta smiled. “Why thank you, Booker. The postman was right. You are a trustworthy big boy.”

“Okay. Gotta go play baseball with my brother.” He ran out the door.

Loretta read the return address. Her heart raced. It was from Jeremiah. She carefully tore open the back flap of the envelope and began to read:

My dearest Loretta,

A year has already gone by since the fire and your subsequent departure from Cape May. As you know from my letters, much has happened here during that year, not the least of which is that I have grown to miss your presence more and more each day. I trust that you are well and prospering in your job and your home.

You will love the new store. It is an even nicer structure than the former one, with more space to add an extra section. There is also a lovely, modern apartment on the second floor.

The only thing missing is you. If you could find it in your heart to return, I would be delighted to offer you your old job once again. But this time, I would like to offer it to you as my wife. Furthermore, there is enough space in the building for you to open your own knitting shop, if such a venture would still interest you.

I trust you will not consider my method of proposing to you an obnoxious one, but given the miles that separate us, I had no other choice.

I love you!

Jeremiah

Shaking with sobs of utter joy, Loretta clutched the letter to her chest. The words she'd longed to hear she'd finally heard.

"Yes!" She shouted her response at the top of her lungs, as though Jeremiah could hear her across the miles. "Yes, Jeremiah Collins! I accept your marriage proposal! I accept it with all my heart!"

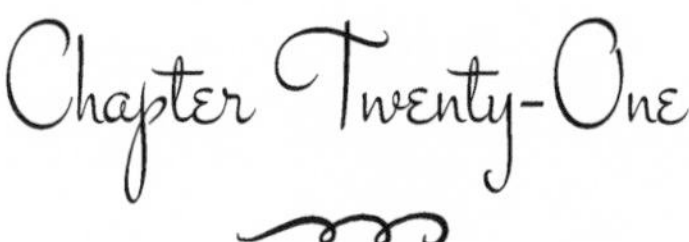

Chapter Twenty-One

Loretta ran into Miz Abigail's kitchen, still holding Jeremiah's letter in her hand.

The elderly lady stood at her stove, cooking fried chicken. The aroma made Loretta's mouth water as the bacon fat crackled in the frying pan.

Mis Abigail turned toward Loretta. 'Whatcha got there, chile?"

Tears welled up in Loretta's eyes. "He asked me to marry him."

Miz Abigail broke into a big smile. "I knew it was just a matter of time." She put the lid on the frying pan and lowered the heat. "Let's sit down a bit."

Loretta pulled out a chair for Miz Abigail and then sat down beside her. "I don't think I've ever been so happy in all my life."

The creases around Miz Abigail's eyes and mouth deepened. "Love be the most powerful emotion of all." Her face softened and her gaze grew distant. "I remember when I first met Pastor Perry." She shook her head and chuckled. "Oh, was I impressed!" She looked straight at Loretta. "The Lord done blessed you."

"I know. I think this marriage will be far better than my first. At least, my husband won't be off traveling all the time." Bitterness edged her voice.

Miz Abigail's gaze studied her. "Have you forgiven your first husband?"

Her question took Loretta aback. "What do you mean?"

"I mean, have you forgiven him for not bein' there for you while he was alive, and for leavin' you penniless after he died?"

Loretta searched her heart. Truth be told, she still harbored rancor toward Edward. He'd put her through suffering no wife should have to go through. Just thinking about it still upset her.

Miz Abigail tilted her head. "Well, chile, have you forgiven him?"

Loretta had to be honest. She shook her head. "No, Miz Abigail, I haven't."

"Then you must, chile. You must. Unforgiveness

has a way of eatin' at the heart—and at the body, too, I might add. So many be sufferin' from all kinds o' ailments 'cause they're carryin' around unforgiveness in their hearts."

"But Edward ruined my life. How can I forgive him?"

"How can you not?" Miz Abigail placed a hand on Loretta's. "Chile, if the good Lord has forgiven you, how can you not forgive another?"

Loretta stiffened. "I'm not God, Miz Abigail."

"No, chile, you ain't God. But He done given you the grace to act like Him."

"But I still feel anger toward Edward."

"Loretta, hear me now. Forgivin' ain't about feelin'. Forgivin' is all about decidin'. We choose to forgive by an act of our will. When we do, eventually the bad feelin's change into good ones."

Loretta lowered her eyes. "You make it sound so easy."

Miz Abigail's eyes filled with compassion. "Obeyin' God ain't always easy. Most o' the time, it's hard. Real hard. But when you love God more than you love yourself, it gets easier."

Miz Abigail's words pierced Loretta's heart. Who was she not to forgive Edward when God Himself had forgiven her? Did she think she was better than God?

He alone knew Edward's heart, and He alone could judge it. Not to forgive Edward would be to usurp God's position and to make herself God. It would be nothing short of idolatry. The very thought struck fear into her heart.

Loretta swallowed hard. She looked at Miz Abigail. "You're right, Miz Abigail. I must choose to forgive Edward, no matter how difficult it is. I must ask God to forgive me for all the anger and bitterness I've harbored in my heart."

Miz Abigail smiled. "Then the good Lord done forgive you, chile. He promised in His Word that if we confess our sins, He is faithful and just to forgive us and to cleanse us from all unrighteousness."

Tears welled up in Loretta's eyes. "I feel as though a weight has been lifted from my soul."

"It done has, chile. It done has." She gave Loretta a hug. "Now, you go forth to that new husband of yours. May the good Lord bless you both and keep you in His lovin' care all the days of your lives." Tears glistened in Miz Abigail's eyes.

"I'm going to miss you, Miz Abigail. You've been like a mother to me."

"And you like my very own chile." Miz Abigail wiped the tears from her eyes with her apron. "Now, when you goes back to New Jersey, remember your ole

Miz Abigail an' what she done taught you." She smiled. "And, if the good Lord bring me to mind, say a little prayer for me, will you?"

Loretta's heart warmed. "I most certainly will, Miz Abigail." She gave the dear lady a tight hug.

Miz Abigail took both of Loretta's hands. "Lord willin', chile, we get to see each other again this side of heaven. If not, I'll be seein' you on the other side."

Loretta could no longer contain the bittersweet tears that flowed freely from her heart. Tears of sorrow at leaving Miz Abigail and Amazing Grace Church—and tears of joy at rejoining Jeremiah.

A few days later, while sitting on the porch of his new building, Jeremiah received a telegram from Loretta. His heart trembled. Had she accepted his marriage proposal, or had she refused it?

His hands shaking, he tore open the sealed flap.

My Dearest Jeremiah,

You have made me the happiest woman in the world! I gladly accept your proposal of marriage and look forward to spending the rest of my life with you.

I love you!
Loretta

A cry of joy escaped his lips. She'd said *yes*! She'd said *yes*!He stood and shouted to the wind. "She said *yes*!"

A gentleman passing by gave him a strange look and continued on his way.

Bursting with joy, Jeremiah went inside as fast as his bad leg could take him. It was time to turn his store into *Jeremiah's Fishing Supply Store* and *Loretta's Knitting Shoppe*.

As a girl, Loretta had always dreamed of a winter wedding. There was something enchanting about bare, ice-covered tree branches that sparkled in the morning sunlight, grass carpeted in snow that reflected the purity of the marriage covenant, and long, shimmering icicles hanging from the eaves of the small country church that had embraced her for so many years.

Today, her wish would come true.

Wrapped in a heavy, white woolen cape that the ladies of her knitting circle had knitted for her, Loretta walked into the little church in Cape May on the arm of Clarissa's husband, John Steubens. Loretta wondered who was more nervous, she or John.

"Having raised only sons, I've never been father-of-the-bride before." John quipped as they waited in the church vestibule for the pastor's signal to begin their walk down the aisle.

Loretta giggled.

The pastor gave the signal.

Loretta smiled and patted John's arm. "It's time."

As the first strains of Pachelbel's *Canon* began to play, she drew in a deep breath.

This was it. Today was the day she would become Mrs. Jeremiah Collins and begin her new life with the man she loved. Her heart danced at the prospect of spending the rest of her life with him.

As John slowly escorted her down the aisle in tempo with the music, Loretta's breath caught as Jeremiah's gaze fixed upon her. They'd been through a lot together, and those trials had forged a deep bond between them. A bond that would now be sealed with the blessing of God.

Only a few guests occupied the wooden pews on either side, those closest to Loretta. Molly, a radiant smile on her face, stood in the frontmost pew on the left, flanked by Sean, also smiling, a protective hand upon his wife's shoulder. Loretta's heart soared.

Behind Molly and Sean, the ladies of her knitting circle filled the entire row. Ebony and her husband Marcus. Miriam, widowed only two years earlier. Cholena, with her new beau she'd met at camp meeting. Ornella and her husband Giuseppe. And Clarissa.

John stopped in front of the altar and gently transferred Loretta's hand from the crook of his arm to Jeremiah's. The warmth of Jeremiah's hand over hers settled her into deep joy.

As she spoke the words, "I do," Loretta locked eyes with Jeremiah's. In their deep pools, she saw her own reflection. The reflection of a woman who had grown from dependence, through independence, and, finally, into interdependence, the highest form of relationship.

This was where she belonged. This was where she would stay. This was where God wanted her to be.

And, in the end, that was the only thing that mattered.

Loretta stood behind the counter of her new knitting shoppe. Jeremiah had added the extra space during the rebuilding process, hoping it would be a wedding gift to her. A gift she would cherish all the days of her life.

Loretta laughed as Ebony, Miriam, Cholena, Ornella, and Clarissa browsed around the shop, chatting excitedly over the varied items available for sale. Not only were there knitting needles and many types of yarn, but Loretta had also expanded her offerings to include embroidery and cross-stitch supplies. There was a veritable storehouse of wonderful items from which to choose.

"Oh, Loretta! I am so excited for you." Cholena placed several skeins of brightly colored yarn on the counter. "This is a miraculous answer to prayer."

Beside Cholena stood a kind-looking gentleman whose eyes were glued to her. Cholena turned toward him and blushed. "Loretta, I'd like you to meet my fiancé, Richard Bowman."

Loretta's heart rejoiced. "I am so happy to meet you, Mr. Bowman. You have chosen a very fine woman to be your bride."

He nodded sheepishly. "Yes, she is most certainly an answer to prayer."

Cholena beamed. "And an answer to mine as well."

Loretta clapped her hands. "Praise the Lord!"

Tears filled Cholena's eyes. "I am so happy for you, Loretta. Standing in your new shop reminds me that dreams do come true."

"This knitting shop was originally your idea, Cholena. Do you remember?"

"Yes, I do. It seemed far-fetched at the time, but God's ways are far above our ways."

Loretta tallied Cholena's order. "When is the big wedding day?"

Cholena's face glowed. "We're planning to be married in early fall."

"Oh, Cholena. I am so very happy for both of you."

Clarissa stepped up to the counter. "With such wonderful answers to prayer, perhaps we should change the name of our knitting circle to *The Wives of Old Cape May Knitting and Prayer Circle*?"

Loretta laughed. "I like that, Clarissa. It would certainly embody who we are."

Ornella came up to Cholena's side, her little girl toddling at her side. "Loretta, I am so excited I don't know where to begin. There are so many beautiful yarns from which to choose. I will be knitting clothes for my children for the next several years." She, too, had several items in her shopping basket.

The little bell above the door tinkled as several new customers entered. One by one, they expressed delight and gratitude at having a needle arts supply store in town.

"This is such a wonderful addition to Cape May's downtown area." An elderly lady smiled. "I guarantee that when customers get wind of your shop, they will flock from far and wide."

Loretta's gaze scanned the precious women before her, every one of them a treasure to the Lord. Henceforth, she vowed to spend the rest of her days being about God's business as she ran her own business.

She would help each woman who walked through her door understand a little more that she was created by God on purpose and for a purpose. And, as the

Holy Spirit led, she would help each woman discover what that purpose was.

THE END

Author's Note: If you enjoyed this book, please leave a review on Amazon, Goodreads, and/or BookBub. Reviews help readers make wise buying choices, and they help authors get the word out about their books. Thank you!

Acknowledgments

No book is written in isolation. All books represent the joint efforts of many people. This novel is no different.

I would like to express my deep gratitude to the following people who provided valuable research information and moral support during the writing of this story.

First, my heartfelt gratitude goes to my Lord and Savior Jesus Christ and His Holy Spirit. Thank You for trusting me with the story of Your heart.

Next, my deep love and respect go to my awesome husband Dom who prayed me through this book, who did the grocery shopping, the cleaning, and the cooking while I spent time in the "zone." And, after all that, he did a thorough edit of my manuscript, reading through it several times. His attention to detail, his understanding of cause-and-effect, and his meticulous research contributed greatly to the historical accuracy of this story.

My precious daughters, Dr. Lia Diorio Gerken and

Gina Diorio Pope, encouraged me along the way through their love, their humor, and their prayers. Without question, I have the best daughters in the universe.

My deepest gratitude also goes to my powerful prayer partners who prayed with me through each obstacle that came against the writing and publishing of this story. I would especially like to thank Sandra Marrongelli, Dr. Adeola Akinola, Devata White, Barbara Hart, Christine Strittmatter, and Joan Gangwer. Your prayers helped birth this story. Thank you!

Thank you to my amazing beta readers—Glenda Dixon, Christine Pleiman, and Yvonne Gilbert—who took precious time out of their busy lives to read and offer valued comments on my story.

Thank you to my awesome Diorio Champions, the best reader team a writer could ever ask for.

Thank you to editor *par excellence*, Denise Weimer, who edited my story as though it were her own. What more could an author ask?

Finally, thank you to Mr. Mark Seiderman of the National Oceanic and Atmospheric Administration (NOAA) for his expert help on a climate question for Cape May, NJ, in the late 19th century, and to Mr. John Corbett, Mr. Bob Chaulk, and Ms. Lynette Richards of the *SS Atlantic* Heritage Interpretation

Park in Halifax, Nova Scotia, for their outstanding help in verifying facts about the worst maritime disaster of the nineteenth century. Your help was invaluable in contributing to the historical authenticity of this story.

About the Author

MaryAnn Diorio writes riveting women's fiction from a quaint Victorian town in southern New Jersey, not far from the Cape May of this series, where neighbors still stop to chat while walking their dogs, houses still sport wide, wrap-around porches, and the charming downtown still finds kids licking lollipops and old married couples holding hands. A Jersey girl at heart, MaryAnn is a big fan of Jersey diners, Jersey tomatoes, and the Jersey shore. You can learn more about her at maryanndiorio.com.

Other Fiction by MaryAnn Diorio

The Madonna of Pisano
A Sicilian Farewell
Return to Bella Terra
In Black and White
Miracle in Milan
Surrender to Love
A Christmas Homecoming
Fire-Engine Love
The Antique Clock
Dixie Randolph and the Secret of Seabury Beach
Penelope Pumpernickel: Precocious Problem-Solver
Penelope Pumpernickel: Dynamic Detective
Penelope Pumpernickel: Mystery Maven
Miracle at Madville

MaryAnn's books are available at maryanndiorio.com/book-table and on Amazon, Apple Books, Barnes & Noble, and Kobo, and wherever books are sold.

How to Live Forever

Eternal life is a free gift offered by God to anyone who chooses to accept it. All it takes is a sincere sorrow for your sins (contrition) and a quality decision to turn away from your sins (repentance) and begin living for God.

In John 3:3, Jesus said, "Unless a man is born again, he cannot see the Kingdom of God." What does it mean to be "born again"? Simply put, it means to be restored to fellowship with God.

Man is made up of three parts: spirit, soul, and body (I Thessalonians 5:23). Your spirit is who you really are; your soul is comprised of your mind, your will, and your emotions; and your body is the housing for your spirit and your soul. You could call your body your "earth suit."

When we are born into this world, we are born with a spirit that is separated from God. As a result, it is a spirit without life because God alone is the source of life. You may have heard this condition referred to as "original sin." Why is every human being born with a spirit separated from God? Because of the sin of our first parents, Adam and Eve.

I used to wonder why I had to suffer because of the sin of Adam and Eve. After all, I complained, I wasn't even there when they ate the apple! Yet, as I began to understand spiritual matters, I began to see that I was there just as a man and woman's children, grandchildren, great-grandchildren, and so on, are in the body of the man and woman in seed form before those descendants are actually born. In other words, in my children there is already the seed for their future children. In their future children will be the seed of their future children, and so on.

Now, as a parent, I can pass on to my children only what I am and what I possess. For example, if I speak only Chinese, I can pass on to my children only the Chinese language. I possess no other language to give them out of my own self. The same was true with Adam and Eve. Because they disobeyed God, their fellowship with God was broken. Therefore, their spirits died because they were severed from God. As a result, they could pass on to their children only a dead spirit—a sinful spirit separated from God. And Adam and Eve's children could pass on to their children only a dead, sinful spirit. And so on, all the way down to you and me.

We said earlier that your spirit is the real you—who you really are. So what does it mean when your spirit—the real you—is separated from God? It means that unless you are somehow reconciled to God, you will go to hell after you die. Hell is a real place of real torment resulting from separation from God.

Now God is a holy God and He will not tolerate sin in His presence. At the same time, He is a loving God. Indeed, He IS Love! And because He loves you so much, He wanted to restore the broken relationship between you and Himself. He wanted to restore you to that glorious position of walking and talking with Him and enjoying the fullness of His blessings.

But there was a problem. Because God is infinite, only an infinite being could satisfy the price of man's offense against God. At the same time, because man committed the offense, there had to be someone who would also be able to represent man in paying this price. In other words, there had to be a being who was both God and man in order that the price for sin could be paid.

Since God knew that there was nothing man could do on his own to pay the price for his sin, God took the initiative. In the writings of John the Apostle, we learn that "God so loved the world that He gave His only-begotten Son, that whoever believes in Him shall not perish but have eternal life" (John 3:16).

What glorious GOOD NEWS! God loved you so much that He sent His only Son, Jesus Christ, to take the rap for your sins. Imagine that! Would you give your son to go to the electric chair for someone else? Well, that's exactly what God did! The Cross was the electric chair of Christ's day, and God gave His own Son, Jesus Christ, to go to the Cross for you!

In dying on the Cross for you, and in rising from the dead three days later, Jesus paid the price for your sins and repaired the breach between you and God the Father. Jesus restored the broken relationship between man and God. He provided mankind with the gift of eternal life.

So what does all of this mean for you? It means that if you accept Christ's gift of eternal life, you will be "born again." In other words, God will replace your dead spirit with a spirit filled with His life. "Therefore, if anyone is in Christ, he is a new creation. Old things have passed away; behold, all things have become new" (2 Corinthians 5:17).

If I offer you a gift, it is not yours until you choose to take it. The same is true with the gift of eternal life. Until you choose to take it, it is not yours. In order for you to be born again, you must reach out and take the gift of eternal life that Jesus is offering you now. Here is how to receive it:

"Lord Jesus, I come to You now just as I am—broken, bruised, and empty inside. I've made a mess of my life, and I need You to fix it. Please forgive me of all of my sins. I accept You now as my personal Savior and as the Lord of my life. Thank You for dying for me so that I might live. As I give you my life, I trust that You will make of me all that You've created me to be. Amen."

If you prayed this prayer, please write to me to let me know. I will send you some information to help you get started in your Christian walk. Also, I encourage you to do three important things:

1) Get a Bible and begin reading in the Gospel of John.

2) Find a good church that preaches the full Gospel. Ask God to lead you to a church where you will be fed.

3) Set aside a time every day for prayer. Prayer is simply talking to God as you would to your best friend.

I congratulate you on making the life-changing decision to accept Jesus Christ! It is the most important decision of your life. Mark down this date because it is the date of your spiritual birthday. Please write to me to let me know of your decision. I would like to send you a free PDF booklet on how to get started in your walk with Jesus.

Be assured of my prayers for you as you grow in your Christian walk. God bless you!

TopNotch Press

"Putting the heart in books"

maryanndiorio.com